The Inevitable and the Will to Survive

The Inevitable and the Will to Survive

J. William Mac

BALBOA.
PRESS
A DIVISION OF HAY HOUSE

Balboa Press books may be ordered through booksellers or by contacting:

Balboa Press
A Division of Hay House
1663 Liberty Drive
Bloomington, IN 47403
www.balboapress.com
1-(877) 407-4847

Because of the dynamic nature of the Internet, any web addresses or links contained in this book may have changed since publication and may no longer be valid. The views expressed in this work are solely those of the author and do not necessarily reflect the views of the publisher, and the publisher hereby disclaims any responsibility for them.

The author of this book does not dispense medical advice or prescribe the use of any technique as a form of treatment for physical, emotional, or medical problems without the advice of a physician, either directly or indirectly. The intent of the author is only to offer information of a general nature to help you in your quest for emotional and spiritual well-being. In the event you use any of the information in this book for yourself, which is your constitutional right, the author and the publisher assume no responsibility for your actions.

Any people depicted in stock imagery provided by Thinkstock are models, and such images are being used for illustrative purposes only.
Certain stock imagery © Thinkstock.

Printed in the United States of America.

ISBN: 978-1-4525-8046-3 (sc)
ISBN: 978-1-4525-8047-0 (e)

Balboa Press rev. date: 08/19/2013

For my brother Paul, this world could not contain you so it had to stop you.

Prologue

"How did you know what I was going to say?" The woman asked as she motioned to a young lady from across the room.

"Sometimes you just know certain things," I replied. I probably could have explained it to her, but I did not have the patience, nor the amount of time it would have taken her to comprehend. Not that it would have been like trying to explain modern physics to an eight year old. But the amount of time it would take to clarify exceeded the amount of time I actually wanted to spend around the woman.

As the young lady approached me in the crowded lobby of the church, I began scanning the room, much like a computer downloading blueprints of a building. For instance: judging by the vehicles in the parking lot and accounting for all child seats, there were about fifty people in the church. What did this mean to me? If I were dead center of the church and it caught on fire; it would take approximately 7.6 seconds to exit the building, give or take a second or two for severity and direction of the flames.

"Yes ma'am," the young lady said as she reached my side.

"This young man needs to go to the young adult's classroom. Would you mind showing him the way?"

"No ma'am," she answered as she turned towards me. "Hello, my name is Lynn."

I tried my best not to sound too disturbed, but my mind was still scanning the room. Without any warning or disregard for my own idiocy, I just said the first thing that flashed in my mind. "I'd go out the windows . . ." I paused for a moment and mentally slapped myself. "I mean . . . my name is Will."

She was the first person I had met that was my age in weeks. I had spent the last three weeks in jail pretending to be something I was not. I was constantly looking over my shoulder, trusting no one, and ducking or dodging my sanity deprived lethal surroundings. I had no idea what regular teenagers did for their summer vacation, but mine was spent in and out of lockup. I didn't even know how to speak to other teenagers. The only conversations I had in the last few months began with, *"How long are you in for?"* and *"Misdemeanor or felony?"*

"Ok, follow me Will," she said with a strange smirk.

She led me through the main lobby and out the back door. The door opened to what looked like a fungi infested lagoon that did not really inhabit any life forms, other than the seldom mosquito or fly. We walked along a small path of concrete around the building and down to what looked like a shack. The run down storage shed only contained one room, which was packed with a few file cabinets, and a couple of chairs and couches.

As I walked into the class room, I quickly looked the room over and then shut my eyes. I had begun playing this game when I was about seven years old. I would keep them shut, and try my best to remember exactly where everything resided. If I won the game, I would go back to what I was doing. But if I lost, I would walk around the room scanning, until I was sure I would never forget it again.

"What are you doing?" Lynn asked.

"Got it!" I said after opening my eyes and priding myself on a job well done.

"You know, you're kind of weird," she said as I noticed she had that same strange look from before. My effort of trying to blend in was failing miserably.

As the class was about to begin, I eagerly searched for a place to s. I wanted to begin another one of my games called, "people watching." The game "people watching" is a simple game I liked to play; in which you can play by yourself or with countless others. Basically, all you do is watch the surrounding people for reactions and various stereotypes. For example, like she looks like a politician or he reminds me of a prairie dog. It's cheap, it's easy, and it can give you something to do when you are bored out of your mind. I play the game for two reasons. (First, for the unbelievable discoveries of the watchful eye; and secondly, because it is hard to play any other game when no one wants to talk to you).

With an obsessive compulsive fear of not knowing what would be coming, I took a seat in the corner of the room facing the door, and began to play my game. Lynn Todryc, the young lady whom I had already met, is a kind hearted, yet extremely obsessive compulsive high school senior. She is a casual dresser wearing a t-shirt, blue jeans, and a pair of dark green flip flops. She spoke with a soft and pure voice, but her conviction and passion shined through as she answered questions with a direct and reasonable approach. Her stereotype was easy to spot because her down falls were much like my own. She was the caged animal still shaking the cage. Meaning, she was meant for extraordinary things, but for some odd reason she can't find her way out of the cage. It's kind of depressing, considering she was the one who barricaded herself. Plagued with heartache or tragedy, she now contains herself by using cautious reasoning. Something so horrifying, that it ultimately led her down a road, that under the right circumstances, she would have never seen in her lifetime. I'm guessing she had a loss in the family: Maybe a parent or both, a sibling, or maybe even a best friend.

David Daniels, (Lynn's boyfriend) was a bit unconventional. His thought pattern was like no other I had ever saw before. He was more like a genius hidden in idiot's clothing. He could see an entrapment question coming for miles. For instance; in class, the Sunday school teacher said something about evolution and if we believed that we actually came from monkeys. His reply was simply genius, yet stupid at the same time. "Let's say that we did come from monkeys. They are just as smart as we are and they can do everything we can do. If that is all true and if we put toilet-paper in every tree in the jungle, they would they begin wiping their own butt's?" His statement was stupid because of obvious reasons, yet intelligent for the sole purpose of his humor allowing him to evade his true beliefs. I thought it was a bit strange that he and Lynn were a couple in the first place. They seemed like they were complete opposites. Not in the sense that one was good and the other was evil. But she was uncontrollably serious and passionate, and he did not seem to care about anything, accept for making people laugh. He must have known her before the catastrophe. It seems like his humor is a form of therapeutic retreat, feeding her ability to remember the good times in her life.

As for Laura Maples, the elder lady teaching the class was in her sixties. She has beautiful long brown hair streamed together with a hint of grey and white. Most women at her age would dye the color, but she carried herself in such a manner that it was more like a badge of honor. When she spoke, she seemed informative; not all knowing, but experienced nonetheless. With consummate eye contact and empathy for everyone, she focused on every word spoke in class. She even regarded every story with thoughts on her own past and gave examples from the things she saw in her life time. Her exterior was plain to say the least, but her intellect was filled with colorful insight. She was the equivalent of a ballerina, tiptoeing through conversations with grace and attentiveness, but not enough to push anyone over the edge of our so-called "group therapy.

The class began talking about various news stories and how they felt about certain situations. I began thinking about home. I had grown up in a small town in Oklahoma, called Jay. Life there was mellow to say the least. I say this now living in the City of Corpus Christi, Texas. Jay and Corpus Christi are completely different. In Jay we didn't have drive by's; we had brawls or fist fights at the local lake, where everyone went home afterwards and slept it off. We didn't have cell phones; we had one land line for each house (if you were lucky to even have that.). We didn't have shootouts with the police; we had shots with the local sheriff and deputies. And we didn't have countless restaurants or outlet malls; we had a diner and a tractor parts store. Our small community looked rough and tough, at least on the exterior, but they were real people. For most of them, there was no hiding their true intentions, nor was there really a need for the pointlessness of deceit. It was more of a beautiful setup for a give and take society. For if anyone ever needed help, there was always someone around to lend a hand. When I was younger I dreamed of moving away to the big city, but now that I actually live here, to be completely honest, I miss being home.

"How do you feel about it Will?" Mrs. Maples asked.

I thought for a moment about what the group had been talking about as the question resonated in my mind, *"How do you feel about death?"*

I had pondered that very question at least a million times before. I have weighed out the options from my belief structure, taking various other faiths into consideration. And after questioning everything I have ever known. I know where I stand in life and I know what I believe the afterlife to be. "To be completely honest, I humbly await its presence," I answered pausing for a moment for a more dramatic effect by gathering their full attention.

As a child my father used to tell me, *"When all else fails try to be honest."* and *"When it comes to something as sensitive as faith and religion in general, you should also remember to be nice."* But on the other hand, I needed a reason to never come back to this place. And it had seemed that I had found my way out in a simple question of conviction. "And truthfully, I'm appalled at the very notion that the people in this very room don't feel the same way. All of you fear even the thought of death and of what is to come. You, the huddled masses of sacred certainty, are no stronger in your faith than the hopeless individuals drowning their sorrows in a bottle of bourbon. I feel like I am surrounded by the infectious outlook of the 'Doubting Thomas' theory. Seeing is believing is the most idiotic thing I've ever heard! You either believe or you don't. I feel ashamed to even think about being affiliated with this congregation and mortified at the thought of what you truly hold sacred. You are a disgrace to the Christian belief and if I had the power I would ban you from the church hence forth!"

With a few heads hanging in shame, and one or two looks of disgust, I turned my attention to Mrs. Maples. She seemed puzzled and maybe even a little distraught. After a few deep breaths she became contemplative. *"I don't know exactly how you knew what we were talking about, considering you've been staring out the window for the last fifteen minutes; but on the other hand, I thank you for your honesty."*

"You're welcome," I said as I leaned back in my chair and continued looking out the window.

"I'm welcome for what?" Mrs. Maples pensively asked.

"You just said, 'you don't know how I knew what you've been talking about, since I've been staring out the window for the last fifteen minutes; but you thank me for my honesty,'" I replied.

"You must be mistaken. I hadn't said anything else to you," she replied with a suspicious look. "And, I was thinking that, I hadn't said it yet," she continued. *"You should stay after class!"*

"That's what I heard. Whether you thought it or said it. Does it really matter," I snapped back, now becoming angry, "And yes, I'll stay after class, but for today and today only!"

"Please stop answering my thoughts."

"Fine, I'm done."

"Thank God!" She thought to herself.

"Don't thank him, I'm the one stopping it," I laughed.

"STOP READING MY THOUGHTS!!!" She yelled across the room.

"Yes ma'am," I answered.

As the class stared at me wide eyed and speechless, I hoped and prayed that they were stunned from my angered speech. I could really care less if they hated me. But if their silence was from my psychic abilities that always created more unwanted questions. I loathed the average person's telepathic questions, but truly envied their mental capabilities. Needless to say, my abilities were not something I coveted. They were more of the one hit wonders full compellation. You know how you can hear a song for the first time and fall in love with the single. So in an effort to capture more of their brilliance you buy their work in its entirety. Only to realize you hate all their other songs. At the time it seems like it was something you always wanted, only to regret it later.

Growing up in a small town, I had tried my best to keep people from realizing that I was different. My parents had the difficult task of just putting up with me, because I was very quick witted. It must have been hard to raise a child that has an I.Q. higher than both of theirs combined. The only person that could really keep me in check was my brother Eddie. He was older than me, by two years, and a constant thorn in my side. But I needed him in my life, if only to keep me on track. We actually were the precise equivalent of good and evil.

We were akin on intellectual insight, but complete opposites in our intentions. Our constant questioning of the others actions, helped to keep us focused. Although Eddie was a great person at heart, he also had his own shortcomings, but I loved him all the same. In the end, he was my hero and mentor.

"Look, I'm sorry for interrupting the class," I said as I saw the last person walk out of the room, "I promise it won't happen again and I'll even give you my real answer to your question. The fact is nothing about life and death really matters, except for the departure's mark that they leave behind. Stressing over life after death only hinders the outcome of leading a good life and leaving a positive signature on existence itself."

"You're not reading my thoughts right now, are you?" Mrs. Maples asked.

"It's more than just reading thoughts," I replied.

"But . . . how?"

"Look, I don't know you, and truthfully I can't really say that I want to get to know you. So there's no need for me to explain and let you know things about myself that, I wished I didn't know!" I answered.

"William!" My father said warningly as he entered the room, "I don't care what you were talking about," he interrupted me before my rebuttal. "You don't talk to your elders that way!" He continued now turning his attention towards Mrs. Maples. "I'm sorry," he said as he began to calm down. "This is my son, the young man I was telling you about."

As they continued talking, I grabbed my things, and walked out of the room. There was no way I could sit in on another, *"I'm sorry. My son is a little blunt. He's difficult and very hard to handle, ('Oh, poor me,')"* speech; given by my father the symp-a-holic. By the time I was 16, I had heard at least a hundred of them.

"Let's go Will," my father said with a look of disgust as he exited the room.

"Ok, I've come for my one Sunday, of so called 'rehabilitation.' Now will you leave me alone?" I asked.

"No! You're coming back next Sunday, and the Sunday after that, and the Sunday after that!" He snapped at me. "Until you stop being like this, you will come every Sunday, even if I have to drag you kicking and screaming. Also, Mrs. Maples has offered to counsel you."

"Fine," I said shaking my head. I knew that this so-called "rehab," was not going to work; but it was much easier to just agree with him.

"She was going to stay late today but . . ." My father started.

"I know, I know! But, she had to get home to her ill granddaughter," I finished.

"STOP DOING THAT!!!" He yelled. "JUST GET IN THE TRUCK AND SHUT UP!!!"

Chapter 1

As I lay in bed that following Monday morning, I took shallow breathes as I held my eyes closed. Staying utterly motionless, I began to pray that I was dead. "Praying for death, what a conundrum?" I laughed at myself as the sudden painful realization that I was still alive rushed through my mind. I had become somewhat accustomed to waking up at least once a week, from the same ending to every dream. With every dream I had, in the end, the beautiful release of death would come. In this particular dream, I was in some sort of conflict, like a bank robbery or something of that nature. I had my hands tied behind me and I was lying on my stomach. The men in control of the situation entered the room and instantly killed 3 hostages, before getting the young girl next to me. She could not have been any older than 4 or 5. I began begging and pleading with the gentlemen, as I rolled onto my side, to take my life before hers. Although all of these death dreams end in the same manner, the predicament is different in every case. For some odd reason, in the situations that effect more than myself, I find it difficult to watch others die. I don't know why I hold others lives above my own, but it's just a feeling I get when I see others lose their lives. Almost like a gut reaction that makes me believe that I deserve to die. Anyway, now getting back to the dream, as one of the men complied and told me I was next, I rolled back onto my stomach and clinched my eyes shut. For all those people that believe their mind flashes images of their lives before their very eyes. I had nothing of the sort. The blood from the other hostages had now covered the floor, for I could feel the warmth and stickiness on my stomach and face. As a slight feeling of what it was like to drown entered my thoughts, I released a deep breath. As I did, my mind flushed and cleared out even the smallest of thoughts. For once, I felt at peace, for I had no control over what was to come. I heard the gun fire a round and instantly felt a pinch, followed by numbness in the back of my head. My mind went blank as it began to fade into total darkness.

"Still alive!" I thought to myself as I opened my eyes. In most cases people would find these death dreams as a sign to live life to the fullest. All it did was puzzle me to the point of asking why I was still alive in the first place. I realize these are not regular thoughts from a 17 year old, but I'm not a normal teenager.

My name is William Joseph Larson. When I was a new born, my parents realized there was something not quite right about me, because I never cried. I guess my surroundings were deviating enough to keep me distracted, for all I did and continue to do, is learn from anything and everything. When I was 6 months old I learned how to walk. At 11 months I had learned how to talk, and not baby talk mind you, full words and sentences. I learned exponentially. When I was almost 4 years old, I began to see things in my mind. Things I had already seen before. I had discovered my eidetic memory. Although I had already learned so much, my next test would not come for another 4 years, when I had my first déjà vu experience. If I would have known, of what was to come, I would have derailed in hopes of diverging from the path given to me.

"Will, get up!" My father yelled, as he beat on the door. "First day of school and you had better not be late!"

"I'm up," I answered.

My father is an easy man to understand. He is a complacently aggressive fear ridden man. He is so content with where his life is that he pressures others into which direction he thinks their life should be headed. Like a shepherd leading his flock to be sheared. He barks orders, gives direction, and in the end he gets exactly what he wanted the whole time.

Chapter 2

As I pulled into the school, I instantly began to compare it to my old one. It looked more like a college campus than a high school. In my old school, Monday mornings were the worst. Everyone almost seemed like they were dead. Here it could not have been more alive. Friends were meeting up with each other and students were studying. On the grass just to the right of the main doors, there was a small group of people in a pow-wow like setting, conversing about politics, religion, and daily news. I had begun to believe that this school might not be as bad as I had originally assumed. Maybe I could finally have that thrill of being challenged from school work or be mentally tested with the ideas of the cities profound deep thinkers. It was very doubtful, but one could only hope. Even at my old school in my advanced classes, I never felt the luxury of being contested. I would even finish the homework before I even left the classroom.

After a few inept mistakes in the main office, I finally made it to my first class. Thanks to their incompetence, I was already thirty minutes late. As usual I opened the door of the class room and had to play my visual memory game. I glanced quickly, and then shut my eyes. "Can I help you?" I heard a voice say. As I opened my eyes, I became very angry, and made a bee line towards the window directly in front of me. "Can I help you?!?" The voice of the teacher rang a little louder and disturbed this time.

I slapped the schedule in my hand, on his desk, and continued towards the window. "William Larson," he said as I continued to pass him by. As I made it to the window, to my surprise, I saw with my own eyes what I had missed. "Take a seat William," he continued.

I gritted my teeth in anger as I replied to him, "Paperclip!"

"Yes paperclip, very good," he said mockingly. "Next we'll try completing full sentences, now take a seat!"

"Sorry," I replied as I took my seat in the back of the room.

"Of course you are," he said as he shot me a stern look. "Anyway, back to before we were so rudely interrupted."

I did my best and bit my tongue, hoping he would not take it far enough for me to retaliate. Truthfully, I had nothing against the man. I actually kind of admired him. For some odd reason, I like it when someone treats me like I treat the rest of humanity. Yes, he had angered me a little in the way he had conducted himself, but I did interrupt his class. As I stopped my thoughts from stressing the unimportant, I gently closed my eyes, and began scanning the room in my mind. I pointed out everything I could remember, so I would never forget it again. It was also a technique I used so I could defuse. I had always assumed that if I knew where everything was, nothing would surprise me. I was sitting five rows back and three rows in from the door. There were four windows to my left and twenty-nine total desks including the teacher's. There were eighteen students not including myself, and one shady narcissist in the front of the class.

"No! Ms. Trujillo, wrong again!" The teacher barked. "How many times do we have to go over this?"

"Take it easy teach!" I said. I don't know exactly why I had interrupted his class yet again. But it felt like an emotional pull, like I had to say something. It could have been a jealous reaction to the clout that he seemingly had over the remainder of the class; or it also might have had something to do with the puke green shirt he was wearing that set me off. There was really only one way to find out, "Is that the only puke colored shirt you own?" I asked him.

"Shut up, Mr. Larson!" He barked.

"I was right the first time," I told myself.

"You know, I've had just about enough of your interruptions for one day Mr. Larson," he steamed.

"Apparently, you haven't!" I snapped back at him. "Either she had a sudden lapse in memory or she doesn't know! Which only proves that maybe you, as the teacher, should take a different approach! You are not doing anyone any favors by yelling at them or belittling them . . ." I stopped.

As he continued to berate her and I both, with a higher sense of intellect, something finally clicked in my head. His behavior, however inappropriate, was intentional. He had a personal vendetta against this girl. I briefly analyzed the two of them and began riffling through questions to link the two of them together. They couldn't be relatives, they looked nothing alike. There was no comparison in bone structure, eye color, or nervous tendencies. They weren't sleeping together; she was too good for him. At first glance, she looked like a bimbo cheerleader, but her demeanor told a different story. She seemed intellectually equipped, prudently preserved, and at the moment a little frightened. The only answer left was the one I feared the most. She reminded him of the "one" that got away. The sentimental significance was enough to deal with on a daily basis, but now I had caused an eruption of emotion. I needed a truth to defuse the situation. Not something big enough to get him fired, but strong enough that it would cause him to lock up. "How long you been using steroids?" I said taking a shot in the dark. It was merely a guess. I wasn't for sure, but he was a thirty-five year old with oily hair and a severe acne problem.

"That's . . . That's enough!" He replied with a stutter.

Apparently, I was right. His shaky voice was a dead giveaway that he was against the ropes. So I began to lay into him even more. "Let me guess. In high school you flew by because you were a sports star," I guessed again, poking in hopes of finding his reasoning for steroid abuse. "Even if you didn't make the grades to play, they would give them to you anyway. Then you didn't score high enough on the A.C.T.'s to get into a credible college. So you thought 'why not go to community college and then transfer?' Before long, college turned into drinking heavily, and partying with friends," I continued. I couldn't control myself. It was as if I could hear every word that was about to slip out of his mouth. And every thought he had, had condemned him a little more, as true facts of this man's own life began rolling off of my tongue. "Eventually you ended up graduating at the bottom of your class. But then all the good jobs were taken, by your fellow classmates who actually worked hard. Not too long after that, one drunken rage turned into one too many and you decided it was your last resort, to become a teacher."

"Enough!" he yelled across the room. I had done my job. I had left him in the same state of mind that he had left the young lady, speechlessly dumbfounded and ashamed.

As I stopped, I realized that it had all started again. I was sticking out like a sore thumb, as usual. Everyone in class was staring at me, just like yesterday in church and before that, in Jay. This was supposed to be my new life, where I wouldn't make the same mistakes. Luckily, I became distracted with the bell ringing for the end of class. Although class had ended, everyone was still sitting in their seats, caught in an unbelievable limbo of sorts. So I quickly said the first thing that came to mind, "So . . . How about this weather we've been having? Crazy isn't it?" As I began to notice that no one had even budged, I quickly grabbed my things and rushed out the door.

I tried my best to remain secluded for the rest of the day, but you don't always get what you want. As I stepped out of the back of the school, to begin my new ritual of drinking a pint of whiskey before the lunch hour was over, I quickly opened the container and took a drink. It only took a few seconds to remember that I didn't really like to drink. Slowly and coercively I mentally prepared myself for the remainder of the poison I was about to consume. I forced myself to push back thoughts, like my father's whole side of the family being nothing but addicts, and convinced myself that I didn't really have a choice in the matter. I needed to drink to keep my mind on idle. As I tipped the bottle up, I heard a voice come from behind me, "What are you doing?"

"Trying my best to drink away some memories," I said with my back still to her. "And what brings Ms. Elizabeth Ann Trujillo out here?"

"I just wanted to thank you for what you did in class earlier. Wait . . ." She paused for a moment. "Do I know you?"

"No, but I know you," I answered. "You're a Senior, 5'6", hazel eyes, with golden blond hair, and a twenty minute tan from surfside tanning salon. You're wearing a red pull-over, blue jeans, and black flip flops." I continued with my back still to her.

"Anything else?" She replied as I finished the bottle.

"Yes," I said as I wiped my mouth clean and put the cap back on the bottle. "Your favorite color is purple, but you only think you look good in red and pink, so that's all you wear. You spend your extra time feeding the homeless," I said as I tossed the bottle into the parking lot. "You love romantic movies and sometimes you can't control how excited you get when you see puppies," I said mockingly.

"Um . . ." She began.

"Look," I stopped her refutation. "I can literally do this all day. I don't care who you are or how wealthy your family is. I could care less about your feelings and I certainly don't give a crap about how grateful you are. So please, go back inside, and leave me alone."

As I turned around to look at her, I expected many things; like an angry face and a furious storm off. But instead, I looked into the eyes of a tearful, mind cleansing, soul quenching angel. My mind shifted for a moment and shot a sharp pain through my head, only stopping to etch out the vision of her that I had just received. "My turn," she said. "You're Will Larson, aside from being the most outspoken person I've ever met. You're about 6'3", blue eyes, the darkest soul I've ever seen, and by far the biggest prick I've ever known . . . I'm sorry. I can't do this," she said as she turned around and headed back into the building.

I had the instant feeling that I had been sucker punched. "What the . . . ?" I gasped. With every word she said, it seemed like it killed me a little more inside. My eidetic memory had taken those unforgettable sentences, and bore them into my head. I continuously heard them over and over again as they turned into a nauseating high pitched squeal, followed by her imprint that was recently engraved in my head. Again and again, the sounds echoed in my head as a light shined with every heart beat on the visual outline of her face. I stood there for a minute, just waiting for the stinging to stop, as I prayed for it to fade.

With my first day of school in the books, I now walk the beach in hopes that my father will fall asleep soon. My bad luck from that day, continued on unto the night. The school had called and told my father about what had happened in class that day. He became angrier as

I tried to explain to him that it was not my fault. Before long the fight became about how much he had to give up when we moved. And I replied with my usual, "Nobody asked you to come! The judge told me to leave, and not come back, not you! You just felt like running away from your problems!"

Anyway, I chose the beach because everyone always says how soothing it is. Well, they lied. My mind ran full blast, ripping through memories, thoughts, and of things to come. I tried my best to focus and then things began to scramble even faster when I lost it. I tried again, and my eyes focused for a moment, on a small group just down the beach. As I strained a little harder, I saw one of them drinking a fifth of whiskey. Without any hesitation, I quickly began running towards the bomb fire that they surrounded. "Hey, aren't you that new kid?" The man said as I took the bottle out of his hand. The more I drank, the more everything began to slow down. Before I knew it I could see again and I began to focus on the people around me.

"Yeah, I'm the new kid," I answered.

"Everyone said you were kind of weird." He said as I tossed the bottle into the ocean.

"Awesome," I said mocking him. "Well everyone says you're a simple minded Neanderthal that crawled out of his hole to sponge up all the intellect in the world, so your idiocy would allow you to fit in. Why even try? You don't understand any of this. Do you?" I do not know exactly why I said that last statement. Even as I was saying it my mind was instantly thinking, *"Who's saying that?"*

I felt a breeze from his arm when I ducked his right hook. And I couldn't help myself but to giggle a little and smile, as I folded my hands behind me. It was like a game between him and I called "See if you can hit me." I could have hurt him if I wanted. On many different occasions where he had left himself open for a hook to the left side of his face or an uppercut to the midsection. But I needed to get into their little clan. This was more like an effort to gain an interview. The fight would not last long anyway. He was a strength fighter. Strength fighters only care about one thing, ending the fight quickly. They have no stamina for long drawn out tussles. Hence, shortly thereafter, he began calming down and finally stopped swinging all together.

I spent the rest of the night getting to know my new friends. Matt, the so-called brains of the organization, was a 19 year old meth-head. He was a bit wishy washy. He seemed like a big mouth but a bit paranoid at the same time. He told me how he was the biggest dealer this side of the harbor bridge. In Corpus Christi, that was a pretty big landscape, about 75 square miles. Then he began contradicting himself, when he said he never crossed the causeway, he just stuck to the island and Aransas pass. I had the distinct feeling that he didn't have the slightest idea of what he was talking about. His incoherent babble made him hard to communicate with, but easily influential, making things easier in the long run.

Matt kept two goons with him at all times. Steve, the know it all, didn't trust me and I could not say that I blamed him. He had just met me that night and his so-called "boss" was acting like I was an old relative. Steve was a "live in the grey" type of person, on top of being very shadily crazed. For example: If you asked him for help, and if he agreed, you could depend on him. But he might also crack you over the head with a lead pipe, just to see if you bleed like everyone else. Such as a man that would steal your wallet and buy you lunch with your money just because you were having a bad day.

The other was Sean, the ape like creature that I had taken the bottle from. As tough as he looked, he was an even bigger teddy bear. He definitely was not one of the smartest creatures God had created. For instance, for some odd reason he was convinced that he had an IQ of 20/20. But altogether he had a good heart, for he saved me from stumbling into the fire, not but ten minutes after our little fight. Sean was the fall guy for the group. He was reliable in the sense that you could count on him to never use up the supply. But if the faction was ever pinched, Sean would be the person everyone would roll over on to keep themselves out of prison. I didn't think that anyone would ever buy that Sean was a master mind behind a drug industry, but something like this happens more often than one might think.

Lastly Matt's biggest dealer, for he was the only one still in school, was David. The very kid I had met in the church the day before. "You can tell you're not a local. We like to try to keep our beaches clean around here," David said after fetching the bottle I had thrown into the ocean. It took him twenty minutes to find the bottle, but apparently it was worth it to him. "What are you doing out here?"

"Getting some fresh air," I replied as I began to walk back to my truck. I had noticed that my buzz was beginning to wearing off, and my headache was about to finish what it had already started earlier that night. By melting what was left of my brain.

"You don't need to get wrapped up in this kind of stuff," he said as he began to follow me to my truck.

"Look who's talking! For one, I know what I'm doing. And two, last time I checked you're not my father," I said as I opened the door of my truck. "And even if you were. I'd tell you the same thing I tell him, when he tries to give me his, 'good advice speech.'"

"I get it," he stopped me.

It must have been his surroundings and supporting cast leaving David in a discomfort zone or something. He didn't seem to be his usual self. No snappy comebacks or stupid stories. Not that I really cared all that much about what he thought or did. I mean, who did he think he was? Telling me what I should and should not do? Needless to say, regardless of David's feelings in the matter, I drove home not thinking twice about him or his opinions.

Chapter 3

The following Sunday was brutal. I sat in the class room, much like I had spent the last week, hiding from everyone. I stayed as quiet as I possibly could and began to hope it would all end soon. Not that I was looking forward to my conversation with Mrs. Maples after class, but I just wanted it over with. I couldn't wait to go home, just so I could pray that I wouldn't wake up the following morning. *"With my frequent death dreams, it could only be a matter of time,"* I thought as I smiled a little.

As the class room deliberated, I sat in my now usual chair. I wondered for a moment, how much more I would actually take of being poked and prodded mentally by Mrs. Maples. Before it became annoying and led me to begin lashing out?

"So your father says that you moved down here because of a little trouble you got into in Oklahoma?" Mrs. Maples asked.

"Do we really have to do this?" I questioned.

"He also said you had a hard time dealing with your parents' divorce . . ." She continued as if I had said nothing.

I had hoped that my father had said nothing to her. I knew now that he must have told her everything. Any and everything that he thought might help her in her journey into my mind. "I'm not doing this . . ." I started.

"And your father also added that your brother Eddie might have had a hand in your problems."

I sat in astonishment, as cold chills ran up my spine and a few emotional visions bombarded my mind. It was nearly a miracle in itself that my father had even spoke Eddie's name. With everything that had happened in our family, Eddie had become a touchy subject. So much that no one felt the need to even say his name. It felt as if everyone had begun to believe that Eddie had never existed at all. *"Apparently it's easier to forget, than to overcome,"* I said to myself as I quickly took a moment and back tracked to the last time I saw Eddie.

Two months after our parents had split up; Eddie and I were in his new apartment. I was staying there for a couple of days while, for some odd reason, both of our parents were out of town. Eddie and I had become very close, especially since the fighting between our parents had begun. We decided it was an, "us against the world situation." Eddie had just asked me to move in with him and I had answered, "Please and thank you." We both knew that it would only be a matter of time before I was out of the house as well. My parents were usually busy and it seemed as if they could care less about me. They were always busy fighting over who got what and whose fault it was that they had split up in the first place. For the first few weeks, I had the distinct feeling that my parents could not stand me. Then I turned into nothing more than a shadow on the wall, or a hint into a past life between the two of them that they wanted to forget. Anyway, without Eddie in the house, I had no outlet for my intellectual thoughts. With a deepening sense of abandonment, I began sneaking over to his apartment almost every night.

I remember after Eddie had asked me to move in, his phone rang. As I waited for Eddie to get off the phone, I thought about how much had changed from when we were kids. Eddie had gone from the jerk that lived down the hall, to my best friend. After discovering that he and I both had an unusual talent for memory, Eddie began to test himself daily. Seeing what his limitations were, I guess. Somewhere along the way I was pulled into it as well. When his challenges got too hard and I wanted to give up, he would push me even harder. Eddie was a born leader and refused to give up on anything. "Gifts like ours are not given out to random people," he told me as I pushed to complete my daily challenges. "Nor are they handed out every day. They're probably not even handed out in a lifetime. We have these abilities for a reason, reasons beyond our own knowledge. Nonetheless, we have a destiny and it is left up to us to fulfill or abandon it. Make your decision!"

I thought it was a little too much of a dramatic approach to tell me these things, while we did vertical push-ups and I repeated every word he said back to him in Spanish. A language I had only learned twenty minutes prior to his speech.

Along with pushing us to the limits, it had seemed that Eddie had gone on some sort of religious kick. He began coming up with these new sayings and phrases. They were very clever, but they also really ticked me off. His favorite was, "Many will pray and ask for Gods help, but very few will accept the journey provided from him to attain it." Truthfully, I didn't remember asking for anything.

When Eddie hung up the phone, he explained that he had to make a trip to Joplin, Missouri. Joplin was about sixty miles away and new home of Eddie's oldest friend, Ben. Eddie quickly grabbed his things and headed for the exit. He looked back as he reached the door, and with a smile he said, "See you later little bro'." The following morning I was awakened to the sound of the phone ringing. It was the police. They needed someone to come identify Eddie's body. He had been in a car accident.

"You don't know anything," I snapped at Mrs. Maples as I tried to fight the tears back.

"So your brother, wasn't a problem for you?"

"No!!!" As the word slipped out of my mouth, it felt like my mind was shutting down. Much like a power outage and now I needed to wait for someone to flip the switch back on. There were no visions or thoughts moving through my mind, nothing. My whole mind went blank as I heard her phone ring. I sat there for a moment, while she talked, and I tried to collect my thoughts.

"What are you doing here?" A voice said as the door opened.

"Oh great, what do you want?" I said as I looked to see Elizabeth at the door.

"Didn't you get enough of a fix the other day?" She asked. "Isn't that how you get your rocks off? Making people feel bad about themselves?"

"Oh, give me a break! I apologized a few days ago," I snapped back. "What more do you want from me?"

"Is it too much to ask for you to fall off of the face of the earth?"

"Will, have you met my granddaughter Eliza . . ." Mrs. Maples chimed in.

"Look, sometimes my mouth out runs my mind," I said. I didn't have the slightest idea of why I was opening up to her, but I couldn't control myself. "I have thoughts that pour in, visions that feel like real life until I wake up, and I usually push people away so they don't see how weird I truly am." After I finished, as if the switch had been flipped, my thoughts and visions began to rush back. The immense flow was excruciating; similar to the pain of holding your head underwater and taking a deep breath.

I heard whispering from the other end of the room, but everything was still indistinguishable. My eyes slowly began to focus, as I saw a semi-blurred visual of Elizabeth and Mrs. Maples talking. "What makes you think I can help him?" Elizabeth asked.

"Because you are the only one he is opening up to. I've been sitting here with him for a half an hour and got nothing out of him." Mrs. Maples replied, with a hopeful smile.

"But grandma . . ."

"Please, put yourself in his shoe's . . ." Mrs. Maples paused for a moment, as she looked back towards me. My nose had begun to bleed a little and an excruciating pain started shooting through my entire body. "W-Will, are you ok?"

I remember very little of what happened after my eyes rolled into the back of my head. But my unconscious slumber gave me something I hadn't had in a long time, a dream. Dreams were very uncommon or really seemingly unattainable. I believe the last one I had was nearly 8 months ago.

When the dream began, I found myself in a bed, in a house I had never seen before. I suddenly heard a scream coming from outside of the room. I don't know why, but I jumped out of the bed and ran for the door. As it opened, so did my eyes. When I began to focus again, I saw Elizabeth hovering over me. She was staring down at me with tear filled eyes.

"He's not dead is he?!?" She asked, as Mrs. Maples felt for a pulse.

"No, I'm not dead," I replied. "You're not that lucky!"

"Jesus! Will! You scared the crap out of me," Elizabeth said. "I didn't mean to fight with you. This is entirely my fault . . ."

"It wasn't you, this happens quite often," I said as she gave me a worried look.

"Eliza, call 911 . . ." Mrs. Maples said.

"That's ok," I said, shaking my head trying to refocus. "Like I was saying, this isn't the first time it's happened to me." Although it had been the first time I had dreamt.

"Well, at least get him an ice pack for the bump on his head," Mrs. Maples said looking to Elizabeth.

"Here's an aspirin, Will," Elizabeth said. "I'll be back in a minute with the ice pack."

As Elizabeth left the room, my mind settled, and I began to sit up. I had hoped that this kind of thing would not have happened while I was here at the church. "Will, I know you don't really know me or my granddaughter all that well. But, you really opened up to her."

"So!" I waved her on to go ahead and spit out what she was trying to say. I was too busy trying to calm a headache to care about anything else.

While I cradled my head in my hands, Mrs. Maples continued, "I would like to invite Eliza into our meetings."

"I don't think that's a good idea . . ." I stopped. As I thought about it for a moment I realized that I didn't really have a choice. If I grabbed my stuff and headed out the door, I would never hear the end of it from my father. The complicated thing was that I couldn't lie to Elizabeth. I had now seen her on two separate occasions, and when I lied to her, it felt like it was literally killing me. "You know what! Whatever you think might help."

Chapter 4

"Ok," Mrs. Maples said as Elizabeth walked back into the room. "Let's get started."

"Where do I begin?" Elizabeth asked. "I mean, I really don't have the slightest idea of what I'm doing."

"Just ask him any question you want, I'm just here to listen in. Pretend I'm not even here," Mrs. Maples replied.

"Ok," she said as she sat down in the chair opposite of me. Her mind instantly scrambled for the right questions, before she landed on, "On Monday, in the parking lot. You said some things about me that I have never told anyone else. How were you able to do it?"

"It all started when I discovered that I had S.S.T.S.T.," I answered.

"Oh my god, is it contagious?"

"No," I laughed. "I have a photographic memory for: sight, sound, taste, smell, and touch. My brother and I called it S.S.T.S.T. syndrome. We later found out that the conditions scientific name is eidetic memory."

I developed my memory years ago, when I was a kid. I made it stronger from the game I played with my memory, trying to remember where everything was at in every room. After a while my mind began logging all of it, like a computer. When I turned eight, something wonderful happened; at least I thought it was wonderful at the time. I had my first déjà vu experience. For months I tried to figure out where déjà vu came from. Five months later I had a breakthrough. I had a dream about my father trying to wake me up. He was beating on the door and yelling at me to get up. Shortly thereafter, I awoke to my

16

father beating on the door, telling me to wake up. He then opened the door and sat down on the edge of my bed. I do not remember the exact conversation we had, but I had the distinct feeling we had already had the conversation before. From then on, every dream would give me a sense of what was to come. I began every morning by waking up and writing down my dreams. Before I knew it, my mind began logging those images as well. Every once in a while, one or two of them, would come in to play.

The first dream I had that had come true was when I was ten years old. In the dream, I was sitting in a car talking to my mother. I don't know exactly what we were talking about, but it seemed important. She had just flicked the cigarette she was smoking, out the window. And I remember that we were parked in a parking lot. "Now stay here," she said, as she reached into the back of the car for a lunch pail. "I have to take lunch to your father." As she opened the door, I looked out the window in an effort to find my father, and saw nothing but white outside the car. As her car door shut, I awoke.

The following morning, I went to school, and got into a fight with a fifth grade bully. I ran as fast as I could to the nurse's office and faked sick so I could go home. Instantly after picking me up, my mother realized that I was pretending. She asked me what was going on and I told her what had happened with the bully. "You can't just run away every time you have a problem," she told me. "There are people every day that have to do things they don't want to do. You just have to stick in there, everything will work out."

I kind of saw what my mother was trying to tell me. As she flicked her cigarette out the window it finally clicked in my head what was happening. I quickly looked out the window and noticed we were parked in a parking lot. My mother reached into the back seat and grabbed the same lunch pail I saw in my dream. As she turned back towards me she said, "Now stay here. I have to take lunch to your father." What had happened in my dream was coming true. It was winter time and snowing furiously. But as the wind calmed for a moment, I saw my father out in the snow. He was framing up a house. My first vision had channeled exactly what was going to happen, which also taught me a lesson at the same time. I had run away from school so I wouldn't have to deal with a bully. When my father was doing something he didn't want to do either, but did it regardless because it needed to be done.

When I turned about fourteen, I had the visions more frequently, almost daily. Finally, about a year ago, it started an all day thing. Every night, I would go to sleep, and hope to dream. And other than my seldom death dream, it would be exactly what was going to happen the next day.

"So you don't have fantasies when you sleep?" Elizabeth said trying to understand. "Nothing of that nature?"

"No, just images of what is to come," I answered.

"What about these death dreams? What are they like?"

"The last one was only a couple of nights ago. I was standing on the edge of a cliff. I closed my eyes, inhaled a deep breath of air, and took my leap of faith. On my way down I let out a peaceful sigh of relief and embraced the consequences of my actions, but when I hit the ground, I awoke."

"Can you save him?"

"What do you mean?" I replied not understanding the question.

"Can you see everything?" She asked again. "You know from the visions you have every night?"

"No," I said. I don't know why she had asked the question, *"Can you save him?"* But I just let it go. Maybe I didn't hear her right. It could have been nothing more than a random miscommunication. "I can only see what God wants me to," I continued. "And I can only see as much as he/she wants me to see."

"Ok," Elizabeth said. "You've explained enough of your psychic abilities. Now let's put it to the test. How old is my grandmother?"

"She's 63," I said sitting up in the couch.

"Oh, you could have already known that."

"Ok then, how about another one?" I said as I grabbed a piece of paper and a pen. "Write a number on this sheet of paper between 1 and 10." She quickly wrote a number down and sat back waiting for my answer. "I said a number between 1 and 10!" I said as I saw the number in my mind.

"What? Is it too hard for you?" She laughed.

"Fine," I said excepting the challenge. "3,546,239.68, is that good enough for you or do we need to try it again?"

"How . . ." She said with a bewildered look as she unfolded the piece of paper with the same number on it.

"I just told you. Were you even paying attention?"

"Let's keep moving," Mrs. Maples said.

"Oh," Elizabeth said. "Sorry Grandma. So, you believe in God, right?"

"Of course, why wouldn't I?" I complied.

"Well, you seem very knowledgeable. In many ways, with the way you talk, the way you act, and including the psychic abilities. You seem to be more like a genius with every word you say."

I stopped for a moment as I remembered back to a conversation that I had had with Eddie, on that very subject. At a young age I began believing that I was smarter than everyone and could out think anyone alive. Luckily, I had Eddie for a brother. He always had a way to bring me back down to earth. I quickly gave her the same speech that Eddie had prepared for me. "Who is the true genius? The man who knows everything or the man blessed with blissful ignorance? While trying to control everything and stressing over the things he cannot change. The man, who knows everything, will inevitably drive himself insane. When the man who knows nothing, is surprisingly happy with the very little information he does have."

"Ok, genius or not, most people with higher intellects don't believe in God," she continued.

"What most people seem to forget is the natural order of things. Almost everyone believes that knowledge is power. But what they fail to understand is that knowledge also creates doubt. And that doubt is created from the fear of the unknown or something they cannot control. When in reality it all could be subsided by just believing. Having faith and believing in something or someone, greater than one's-self."

"Kind of like a placebo?" She asked still trying to understand.

"In many ways, yes," I answered. "Let me put it this way. Did you know that in the so called beginning days of photography, Native Americans believed that if their picture was taken, that their soul was captured in the photo?"

"Almost everyone knows about that," she replied.

"Exactly, almost everyone knows about it. And to this day, have you ever seen anyone deface their own photograph?

"That doesn't prove them right," she answered.

"No of course not, but just because you don't believe in something, doesn't mean you don't fear the indifferent. The same goes for Witch Craft, Buddhism, or the thought of religion altogether. Anything that differs from your own thoughts and beliefs are frightening. And I believe we act in this manner because nobody wants to be wrong about their faith. Yet in the back of our minds we still fear that we might, which brings me back to my previous point. By having something or someone greater than one's-self, to deal with the insuperable, you can focus on the things you can change."

"So let me get this right," she continued now looking slightly agitated. "You only believe, because it makes it easier for you?"

"Not in the slightest, I have my reasons for faith." I countered back.

"And they are? . . ." she asked.

"Why would I tell you? My reasons are my own. My miracles are not meant for others to decipher and deem legible. I second guess them enough as it is, I don't need help."

"So what, you don't believe in testifying? That's all that it would really be. Testifying a miracle," she urged trying to get me to explain.

"No, I don't believe in testifying, and I especially don't agree with anyone that would testify a miracle. I believe that testifying is not meant for people to brag about their life's phenomena's. It's a secondary tool to clear the air or for self justification into their own actions. Trying to receive confirmation from others about your unexplained wonders could be detrimental to your beliefs. When you empower others in this way you give them the ability to second guess and deconstruct your miracle. Ultimately tearing away a piece of yourself and taking away something that is so emotionally beneficial, it could lead to your demise."

I couldn't believe how much I had opened up to her. I allowed her into my thoughts, deeper than I had ever planned on letting anyone dig. I continually told myself to stop or even think about the ramifications of the information I was giving her, but nothing helped. I began to give her huge chunks of who I was and what I believed. As if I was drugged with some sort of truth serum.

"Why does testifying a miracle have to lead to your demise?" Mrs. Maples chimed in hoping to join the conversation. "Why does it have to lead to something negative?"

There are distinct differences between having a conversation with Elizabeth and Mrs. Maples. Elizabeth will ask questions wanting to understand why I think a certain way. Mrs. Maples is someone that is set in her ways and will ultimately have to be proven wrong to change her mind. I quickly analyzed Mrs. Maples from head to toe searching for her prideful accomplishment. When I stopped I answered, "Your hair looks like crap today!"

"What are you talking about?" She asked as she took out a mirror from her purse and began to mess with her hair.

"Thank you for affirming my point," I answered as she continued to fiddle with her hair. "How much time did you spend this morning fixing your hair, an hour, an hour and a half? You know, I must have seen at least five people complement you on your hair today. And all it took was for me to say one negative thing, and you're in complete disarray. You not only began to second guess yourself, but the five others that have confirmed your achievement."

"William, you don't have to be a jerk to prove a point," Mrs. Maples said.

"Grandma!" Elizabeth replied.

"Well, I'm sorry, but you don't," She continued. "And that still doesn't prove that someone would deconstruct a miracle."

"You're right, it doesn't," I replied as I planned a beautiful setup question. "A man testifies before our congregation. He tells us that he was injured and out of work for a couple of months. Two days after his injury occurred, his wife finds two grand in an envelope in the mailbox. How do you feel about his miracle? And be honest."

"It's a blessing," Mrs. Maples says.

"It seems a bit skeptical, but still a good conclusion," Elizabeth answers.

"A week and a half before the end of my sophomore year, my father fell from a ladder and busted his knee. I spent the remainder of the school year and my summer vacation on the job sight working with my brother. So, to be completely honest, it infuriates me that I didn't receive the same miracle. All it takes is one remark and his miracle would fall apart. I could definitely see myself making a sarcastic assault on his faith, because in the end that is what a miracle is. It is a belief that something miraculous has happened for you. In a matter of seconds, I could completely dismantle his belief structure and with only one question, 'what makes you think you deserve a miracle?'"

"Just because you would do something does not mean someone else would," Mrs. Maples countered back. "This world is cruel, but no one would advertently crush someone else's beliefs."

Our discussion is what I would like to call an entrapment conversation. It was something Eddie and I liked to do to others. We couldn't really do it to each other, because the other would always know where the conversation was headed. But it was a thing of beauty, which caused most people headaches afterwards. "Do you even know how this conversation began?"

"Ah . . . not really," they both answered.

"My opening statement was, 'I believe that testifying is not meant for people to brag about their life's phenomena's.' This is something I believe to be true. Something I have processed and carefully thought out to the fullest extent. But as you stated earlier, 'no one would advertently crush someone else's beliefs.' Which just by uttering the statement you have denied me my own beliefs as if they were merely idea's; causing me to doubt and second guess myself." Of course none of this was true, but she didn't know that. "And believe it or not this is not the first time you have caused me to second guess myself. Last week you asked me how I was able to read minds, which caused me to question my abilities. Are they a miracle from God? Or is it just my eidetic memory reading body language, facial expressions, and listening for change in tone. All the while my mind is rushing through a million possible scenarios, questions, and answers leaving me with a sense of what is going to happen."

My setup was beautifully constructed and carried out perfectly all the way down to the slightest detail. As she began to fumble around searching for the right words to say I stopped her. "It's ok, no need to apologize," I said. I could have acted arrogant, spiteful, and even my more favorable moral value, malicious. But I did not feel the need to be as I continued, "I entangled you in an attempt to stop your attack on my own beliefs. Of course nothing you could really say could cause me to rethink my opinions, but I did this as more of a defensive mechanism. There are more than likely a hundred different reasons why I chose to speak to Elizabeth instead of you. But the biggest reason is, while you both are listening to everything I'm saying; she is trying to learn from me and understand where I'm coming from; and you on the other hand, are waiting for a moment to interrupt for a chance to teach me something. With all due respect, do you honestly think there is something you could teach me that I haven't already thought about at least a million times before?"

"No," Mrs. Maples stopped for a moment soaking it all in. "I guess not. I apologize."

I finished the session up by making a brief statement about whiskey and the stipulations of offline occurrences. But I left out, how if I had done something wrong; such as lie, cheat, steal, or really anything that might be deemed shady. I had to wait for either I do something right, or déjà vu to trigger my mind back on. I didn't want to give her too much information or I would never be able to keep a secret. No one deserves that much power over me.

Chapter 5

The following morning, on my way towards the library before school started, I was still thinking about the conversation I just had with my father. From previous discussions, I knew that the more I tried to explain to my father, the more he became confused and convinced that I was possessed. Our argument was about my deep sleep in the church. In these situations I always found it best just to leave it alone and not make a big deal out of nothing. So I told him that I must have over heated and passed out. I could have been upset that Mrs. Maples told my father about what had happened, but who could really blame her. If something like that had happened to someone else right in front of me, I probably would have acted in the same manner.

As I finally reached the library, I remembered why I liked to head there before class started every morning. Not because I wanted to read a magazine or a book, but because I didn't have any friends to converse with. I knew better than to read in front of people anyway. The last time I read a book in front of another person was in Jay and it was not really reading. My mind more or less scanned the book. I covered 500 pages in nearly 30 seconds. That was how I learned how to defend myself; it was a book on self defense.

As I made my way into the Library, I noticed someone out of the corner of my eye. It was Elizabeth sitting in a corner desk with her head in her hands and a history book next to her. "What's wrong? Lose your lip gloss?" I said with a smirk.

"Shh . . ." She said as she began to get agitated, "I can't find my book bag, if I can't find it, I don't have my home work; if I don't have my home work, I get an F; and if I get an F, there goes my chance to

24

get into a credible college!!! I borrowed the book from a friend, but I don't have enough time to do the work again."

"Ok, calm down," I said as I remembered where I last saw the bag. "Your bag is at . . ." I stopped mid sentence.

"Where?!? If you know where it's at . . . Ah!" She sighed. "It doesn't matter. There's no way I could get it in time anyway!"

"Ok, stressing about it will get you nowhere. First, let's try to remember where you left the bag. Where did you do your home work?" I asked.

"Here at the Library, Saturday afternoon."

"Ok, close your eyes and focus on my voice and my voice alone," I said. "Take big deep breathes and try to calm yourself," I continued as she began to calm down. "Just relax and clear your mind of even the smallest of thoughts. A peaceful mind will help you to think. Now I want you to focus on being here in the library, tell me where you were sitting?"

"I was sitting at the center table. I had just finished my work. I put my things away in my bag and headed out to my car. I drove home and left my bag in the car," she said. "Oh, I left it in my car . . ."

"No," I answered. "Keep going, where did you go next?"

"The next morning, I woke up, and went to meet my grandma at the church . . . I can't do this. Just tell me where it is!"

"You're almost there," I replied. "You've already done all the hard work, just keep going. What happened at the church?"

"I walked into the room . . . and fought with you . . ." Her eyes flew open as she remembered. "I left it on the desk at the church after giving you an aspirin."

"Very good," I said with a smiled. "Now let's do the homework." For her first time, it actually was a good job on her part for tracing back. Most people give up after getting frustrated and demand that I tell them where the object is. The point is . . . that everyone has an eidetic memory. I just use mine more often than others.

"How did you do that?"

"There will be time for that later," I said.

"You know we only have five minutes before class starts, right?" She laughed.

"Good," I said as I grabbed the book. "That's plenty of time." I quickly flipped through the first four chapters and began answering the questions.

Finally after months of being alone and feeling disengaged from nearly everything, I had found someone to connect with. The feeling was short lived though, as I gave her the last answer, we heard the bell ring for the beginning of school.

A mischievous sense of warmth came over me as I stood up and saw David waiting at the doors. Getting into Matt's clique was going to be easier than I had originally assumed. Things were beginning to fall into place. Anxious about what he might want, I told Elizabeth I would catch up to her.

"After my girlfriends little cousin are you?" David said as she got far enough away not to hear us.

"It's nothing like that . . ."

"I'm just kidding peter leach, calm down," David cut me off. "I need your help with something," he continued. "Matt told me to see what you were really made of, that and I don't think I can do this by myself."

David began explaining as the movie of the events began playing in my mind. Apparently, David had met this guy at the beach who seemed interested. So David gave him a sample. A week later, the man came back and bought an eight ball. Three days after that, he came back tweaked out of his mind, wanting more. But he couldn't get the money until this last Saturday. David didn't think it was a good idea, but Matt gave it to him anyway. So now it has been a couple of days and Matt wants his money. I went for the sole purpose of needing an inside man. If my future plans were going to work, I needed David on the inside watching their every move.

"We need to make a stop," I said. I knew doing the wrong thing had its consequences. Every time I lied, cheated, stole, or done really anything that might seem wrong. My mind would power down. The only thing to help me when it powered back up was alcohol. I did not need another day of unconsciousness like the day before.

"Where at?" David asked.

"Liquor store," I replied.

"There's a fifth of whiskey under the seat," he said with a strange look.

"Good, now listen up," I said as I began to explain what was going to happen. "There are two people in the house. What I need from you . . ."

"How do you know that?"

"I'll drop you off around the back of the house," I continued as if he had said nothing. "You will then need to sneak around to the back door. The screen door will be open and if you pull up on the door with the handle before you open it; it won't make any noise. But remember to watch the rake that is leaning up against the back door. It is there for the purpose of alarming them when someone is trying to get in through the back. Try and keep in mind these people are skeezed out of their minds. So be careful and don't make any mistakes. When you get set in place, I'll knock on the front door to get their attention. Right after I knock, you count to three . . ."

"Why three?"

"Because I want them to focus on the front door," I continued. "After you reach three, come around the corner, and shove your shotgun barrel into the face of the guy sitting on the couch. Then signal me by yelling 'FREEZE!' I'll take it from there."

After dropping David off around back, I walked quietly to the front door. I knew as soon as I fired my gun, my mind would flush clear. That means no help, except for my common sense. I continually took deep breathes, calming myself and trying to slow my heart rate, as I began to knock. "Nice and easy," I told myself. "David's life is in your hands, be calm and precise."

As if I saw everything in my mind a million times before, the plan was perfectly constructed and carried out. "FREEZE!" I heard David yell. In my mind I saw the man sitting in the chair, in front of the door, turn towards David. I knew I had to wait for the perfect time to shoot or I would kill the man. "BOOM!" The gun fired in my hand. I stood stunned for a moment as I felt my visions escape me. I heard a scream coming from inside, so I quickly shook my head back into reality, and kicked in the door. As I entered the house, I saw the bullet had done exactly as I had intended. It was precisely .32 seconds after David had yelled.

"Son of a . . . !" The man bellowed, holding his hand.

"Where's the money?" David asked.

"They don't have the money," I answered. "Grab the TV and the DVD player!" I quickly turned my attention to the man on the couch and said, "Give me your gun."

After handing me his gun, I pulled the clip from my own. I discharged the round in the chamber, grabbed the barrel of the gun with my shirt, and wiped it clean. "Take it," I said as I handed him my gun. When the police show up after we leave, it will look like a friendly shooting. With his fingerprints on the weapon, it will be an open and shut case.

"Hey, I got it all," David said.

"Ok," I answered. I removed the bullets from the clip, wiped it down, and tossed it to the man. Yet again, I was trying to cover the evidence with his fingerprints. "Put the clip back in the weapon." I said as he complied. As we heard police sirens nearing I turned towards David, "Wipe the door knob off on the back door, and let's go!"

"Will," David said as we jumped in the truck to head for the nearest pawn shop. "How did you know what was going to happen?"

"So does Lynn know what you do for a living?" I quickly changed the subject. My business is my business. I never tell anyone, anything they do not necessarily need to know.

"No!" He snapped at me. "And I'd like to keep it that way. It wasn't my idea to pull you into this."

"I know," I replied.

"But, I think you should re-evaluate your situation with Matt . . ."

"I think you need to keep your nose in your own business! I know what I'm doing."

David could have said many things after that, but he stopped for a moment and took a deep breath. As he continued he said something that echoed in my mind for hours. While sitting there finishing my whiskey, he said, "If you don't change your mind, you won't change this time." There was no double meaning to the statement. If I wanted things to be different, I needed to make them different. But what David failed to realize, was that the decision was no longer mine to make. I wanted and needed my revenge. I wouldn't rest until I got it. Not only did I hate David for saying what he said. But it also had a lingering effect because it sounded like something Eddie would have conjured up.

"Ok! I can take a hint . . ." He said as if he sensed my anger. "Hey, got a question for you," he said trying to calm me. "What do you get when you have sex with a goat?"

"I don't know," I answered.

"Who cares, you nasty . . . You just had sex with a goat." I couldn't help myself but to crack a little smile. "Look," he continued. "I'm taking the girls to a movie tonight. Would you like to go?"

"Why not," I said as I took a deep breath.

As we pulled into the beach, after going to the pawn shop, I saw Matt sitting on the back tailgate of his truck, with his goons to the left and right of him. He looked like a King, sitting on his throne, awaiting peasant royalties. I stepped out of the truck and dug out the money from my front pocket. "Here," I said as I stepped towards Matt. His goons automatically swarmed just in front of him.

"Giv it ta Shown," he stammered. It wasn't even the middle of the day, and he was already tweaked out of his mind. His face was pail white, and his teeth didn't move when he spoke, much like a ventriloquist. But when he was not talking, his jaw was in constant movement, along with an uncontrollable tongue, continuously licking his lips. He looked like a dog, trying to remove peanut butter from its mouth. "I'll col ya," he continued as his eyes began a constant blink. "In a cuppla days."

"Ok," I answered waving him off and heading back for the truck. "I'll talk to you in a couple of days."

"Don unnermine me!" He snapped at me.

I didn't have the slightest idea of why he was flipping out, but I stood there and took it. It would not be long, before I could get away from this crap for good. *"Only a few more weeks,"* I told myself. *"You're not in striking distance of your goal. Keep your eye on the prize. Your time is coming."*

"Jus do wod I tew ya!!!" He said as he continued to stare me down.

I handed the money to Sean and jumped back in the truck. I would have given anything for my striking moment to be right there on the beach, but now was not the time. His demeanor was leading me to believe that he knew everything, but his stupidity led me to believe otherwise. You see, if he truly knew, he wouldn't try to push me away by yelling at me. Instead he would try to make me happy, so he could keep me close.

Chapter 6

"So you've been hanging out with David quite a bit. Are you into the same things he is?" Elizabeth asked. I had just picked her up from her house and was heading to David's, to meet him and Lynn.

"What do you mean?" I replied trying not to give anything away.

"You know . . . selling drugs?" She asked seeming as if she already knew the truth.

"No!" I scoffed. I had thought about this countless times before. As if I knew the question would ever arise. The only way I can really explain my answer is that she was the closest thing I had to a friend. And for some odd reason, I didn't want to hurt her. Not anymore than I already had. The only problem was that I had lied again. It would only be a matter of time before the visions would set back up and knock me out. All I could do was hope and pray that David had some sort of alcoholic beverage. This whole day was becoming one of those moments, when you look back on it in the future and say, "What was I thinking?" I mean for God sakes! This will be the second time I have been drunk today and we haven't even reached night fall yet.

"Ok, I was just making sure," she said. "With everything that happened with Lynn and her mother . . ."

"What do you mean?"

"When Lynn was 11, her and her mother got into a fight on their way to grandma's house the night before Halloween. Her mother wanted her to dress as a caterpillar and Lynn wanted to dress up as something else, I don't really remember. When they arrived at Grandma's they were still fighting. Lynn said she hated her and went to a room. It was the last time Lynn saw her mother. She overdosed later that night . . . Wait!" She screamed as she clinched the dashboard but it was already too late. I hit a speed bump going 30 MPH and bounced my head off the ceiling of the truck. "Sorry," she laughed. "I forgot to tell you about the speed bumps. Alright, his house is up here on the right," she continued. "About the Lynn situation; I know you don't care," she said as she smiled. "Cyborg's like you don't have feelings. All I'm really asking is that you don't make me lie for you as well."

"Look," I said as I parked in the driveway now rubbing the knot on my head. I wanted to tell her that I wasn't somebody she needed to worry about, because I may be here today; but I may be gone tomorrow. I wanted to tell her that not only did I sell drugs but I also did them as well. But I didn't have the courage to break her heart again. As we made our way to the front door I explained, "Don't worry about me. I'm nothing more than a speed bump on your way through life. Today I'm a conversation about something out of the ordinary and tomorrow I'll be an easily forgotten thought. The three of you will move on to bigger and better things. And I'll still just be that weird kid that no one understands . . ."

"Oh, hey Will. It's a good thing you're here," David cut me off as he met us at the front door and I thanked God for his interruption. "I want to show you my new invention."

David's inventions, much like his mind, were sick and twisted. No one else on the face of the planet would ever think of his disgusting yet intriguing inventions. "Follow me," he said as he led me into the house. We walked down the hallway towards his room and he stopped just before his bathroom. "Now keep in mind, none of my inventions are copyrighted, so don't tell anyone about them."

"I really don't think you have to worry about that."

He opened the door to his bathroom and then stood back for me to notice them. I looked his bathroom over and saw nothing irregular. As I was about to give up, it caught my eye. Above his toilet was a small cabinet. Strapped to the bottom of the cabinet was a pair of metal bars. "So what are they supposed to help you get on and off the toilet?"

"No! You idiot . . . Wait, I mean yes! That's much better than the idea I had for them," he answered.

I knew I was going to regret it, but I asked, "And what exactly was your idea?"

"After Thursday Chili nights, they're here to hold me down," He laughed. "No more squirming across the toilet seat and losing focus from the pain. And I know somebody has already come up with the idea, but mine comes with a complementary mouth piece, for those intense moments."

"You know, with excessive straining, you could blow out your O-ring, right?"

"O-ring, smo-ring," he scoffed. "The O-ring is much like the Easter bunny, Santa Claus, or IRS auditors. They don't really exist. They are just old folk tales people tell to keep others in line."

"Ok, enough," I said as I walked away from the bathroom. "You truly are deeply disturbed. I swear you are the only person I have ever known, that literally causes me pain for trying to understand where they're coming from."

"Thank you," he answered as we walked back towards the living area.

After a few pleasantries of "Hi" and "How are you" in the living room. I sat on David's couch for nearly half an hour waiting for the girls to leave the room. I wanted to give him a heads up that Elizabeth knew his secret. The hardest part of the thirty minute wait was trying to keep my visions at bay. Conversation after conversation I lied about everything. Just to keep them from flooding in and knocking me out. At one point in one of our discussions, I might have even agreed to actually liking the Ballet. I also talked about a girlfriend I had never had that lived in Oklahoma, named Cheyenne. It was probably the toughest thirty minutes of my life. Making up stories on cue and leaving inevitable traps for myself in future endeavors.

When the girls finally left the room, I told him what happened. But apparently he already knew. He began to explain, that the Maple's and Daniel's families have been close friends for many years. When David's mother was out of town, he would stay with Mrs. Maples. One night while he was sleeping over at their house, he was in the living room on the couch. He was trying out a new batch that someone had given him, when Elizabeth walked in on him with a straw up his nose. She didn't ask any questions nor did she wait for him to explain. She just turned around and walked right back to her room. He couldn't complain, apparently she kept it to herself. Because to this day, Lynn still did not know about it.

"Do you have any whiskey?" I asked as I began to search the cabinets in the kitchen.

"No, just beer in the fridge," David answered. "What is it with you and booze? Every time I see you, you're asking for hooch."

"I'm half Irish," I continued to lie as I grabbed two bottles out of the refrigerator. "Drinking, to me, is more like a family ritual! It's more of a way to start things off on the right foot."

"So what did you tell her?" David asked.

"About . . ."

"You didn't tell her, did you?" He replied after I downed the first bottle. "You like her too! Don't you!!!"

"What are you talking about?"

"Don't play stupid. She like's you."

"And how exactly do you know that?"

"Well for one, I have eye's . . ." while he continued talking, I began thinking and drinking the second bottle. He told me that Elizabeth was not the type to just hang out with anyone. She usually kept to herself and strayed away from the outside world. But there was something about me that had her interested. I hoped for my own sake that he didn't have any idea of what he was talking about. For if what he was saying, was true. Then we were about to cross a line, a friend line. Once it is crossed, you can never go back. No matter how hard you try, things will never be the same once you have jumped the border. The border being, boundaries set aside for friends to remain friends. "And for two," he continued. "Who do you think wanted me to ask you to come with us tonight? By no means are we close enough to be friends," he laughed.

"It's not like that . . ." I replied.

"Then tell her the truth. I'm sure she can handle it," he said as I tossed the last bottle in the trash.

"Tell me what?" Elizabeth said as she stepped into the kitchen.

As I turned towards her, I paused for a moment, and took a deep breath. As much as I did not want to tell her the truth, I felt that I

34

needed to. *"Here we go just tell her the truth,"* I told myself. "Nothing," I answered her. *"You coward!"* My mind screamed.

"No really, what do you have to tell me?" She asked.

Before I answered, I quickly grabbed another beer from the refrigerator, and turned back towards her. I would need it because I was about to lie to her again. I tipped the bottle of beer up and began thinking about what to tell her. "I was telling David about how set against drugs I was. Considering my brother died from a drug related incident."

"Oh," she sighed.

"Swing and a miss," I thought to myself. What was I doing? I had my chance to put her in the friend zone and failed to complete my task. She would no longer like me if she knew I was being an idiot. But I also had to keep in mind that if I told her the truth. She could decide to no longer speak to me altogether, which would complicate things at the church. And if she knew I wasn't truly trying to straighten up, it could get back to my father. I know it was selfish of me but other than David, no one else knew. I didn't believe he would ever say anything. Even if he did, unlike Elizabeth, I could live without David.

I tossed the last bottle in the trash and focused back on her. I could almost hear her thoughts screaming at me, *"Go ahead and lie to me, its ok!"*

"You look beautiful," I interrupted before she had a chance to say what was on her mind.

"Thank you," she said.

"Is everybody ready?" Lynn asked as she entered the room.

As we headed to the theater and even during the film, I could not help myself but to think about what had happened earlier that night. Many questions and thoughts began complicating my thought process like: Why couldn't I tell Elizabeth the truth? Even if it got back to my father, when have I ever cared about what my father thought? But there was something else holding me back, something I couldn't explain. The whole night was ruined because I was busy thinking about what to do next. Before long, my misspent youth would catch up to me. My conflict of wanting vengeance would be here shortly. It would probably be best if I kept my distance from Elizabeth and her family altogether. After that night, I vowed to stay away from her but it didn't last long.

Chapter 7

"So you've been dodging me for days, what's going on?" Elizabeth said as she entered the Sunday school classroom for my weekly mental beating. "I thought we were friends?"

I should have explained to her about what had happened earlier that week. With the shootout, the reason I kept my distance from her, and the lying about drugs. But if she knew the truth, she would probably never speak to me again. I don't think I could handle not having someone to talk to anymore. Another selfish act on my part, but for good reason, Elizabeth was an overnight success in my mind. Kind of the best friend I never wanted, yet a feeling of privilege to speak with her. *"As painful as it was to lie to her, it would be even more dreadful to tell her the truth,"* I thought to myself as I remembered back to our first altercation. My half drunken attempt to get her to leave me alone outside the school; and her tearful rebuttal that felt like a flash bomb going off in my head. No thank you. Not again. "I've just been busy," I answered.

"Another week, another breakthrough," Mrs. Maples interrupted as she entered the room. "Let's get started."

"Instead of asking questions this week," I said hoping to keep Elizabeth at bay from asking the question I had been keeping from her for about for a week now. "Would it be ok if I just talked about what I feel comfortable discussing?"

"Sure, of course we can," Mrs. Maples answered.

I began by talking about Eddie and what it was like having him as a brother. Eddie had many down falls when we were kids. But I had to admit, he was the same irritating rash to everyone else. That always made me feel at least somewhat better. I mean, he could have only been a prick to me. But he was never really mean to me in front of other people. Honestly, it was never really an attempt to just be mean. He was more or less just pushing me to excellence.

I followed up with how I had come to realize that Eddie, was eventually murdered. Three days after Eddie had passed. I was lying on the ground at his grave site. I refused to leave and stayed for a total of 78 hours. I was waiting for Eddie to give me a sign of what to do next. I had fallen into a deep sleep and had one of the craziest dreams I had ever had. I dreamt that I was in the car with Eddie, on the night of his death. I smiled for the first time in a long time, just because I saw his face. I felt a comfortable peace flush through my mind. For some odd reason, I believed everything was going to work out exactly like it was supposed to. I believed I was going to die in the car with Eddie. As I looked away from him, into the rear view mirror, I saw a car behind us. The car looked familiar, but nothing registered in my mind of who it was. Before I even had a chance to think, I felt the car nudge us from behind. As we eventually lost control of the car, we spun into a tree at about 80 MPH. When the car struck the tree, I awoke.

I assumed that it was nothing more than a dream. After a few minutes of collecting my thoughts, I decided it was time to go home. Eddie wouldn't want me to linger around his eternal resting place for the rest of my life. I said my final goodbye's and left the cemetery. When I finally made it home I checked the rear bumper of Eddie's car, just to see if I was going crazy. Just like I had seen in the dream, there was a black smudge on the bumper. I never saw the marking before. And with my obsessive compulsive memory, I couldn't deny the facts I had been shown earlier that morning.

As the story came to a close and while awaiting yet another question, I looked over to Elizabeth. She was sitting back in her chair with her eyes now welling up with tears. It was as if she shared my pain in some strange way. "I'm so sorry," she said trying her best to contain herself.

"It's ok," I said trying to calm her.

"What kind of trouble did you get into that made you leave Oklahoma?" She asked. She was continuing and trying her best to stay focused on the task at hand, but it was hard when she had to keep wiping the tears from her eyes. Was it anger I was beginning to feel? Or maybe I was just feeling a bit defensive from the things that were beginning to change? Things that I didn't necessarily want to change but apparently it was time; for I couldn't stop myself. Her loving demeanor was a warm, comfortable, and peaceful spiritual lifting that I longed to embrace. It was a non-comparison shift from the cold, irritating, and chaotic life I had led up to this point. Confused and maybe even a little distraught, I continued.

After learning the truth behind Eddie's accident on that fateful night, I began my search in Eddie's phone records. I needed to know who Eddie had spoken with that night, before he had jetted off to Joplin. As I filtered through his records I saw the only phone call within a twenty minute interval of him leaving his apartment. The call came from his friend Ben.

Eddie's reason for leaving was because of his side job, which he never told me about. Not to say that I did not know about it, but Eddie had begun dealing drugs. I couldn't blame him, it was quick and easy money. Which he used to help pay for his new apartment. He would travel back and forth from Joplin, sometimes 2 to 3 times a week. His connection into his extracurricular activities was his friend Ben Staul.

Ben was Eddie's closest friend. In high school, they were on the debate team together. One day Eddie walked in on Ben smoking methamphetamines out of a piece of tinfoil with a straw. When Eddie asked what he was doing, Ben replied, "getting prepared for war."

Every night before a big meet, Ben would freak out a little and stay up all night studying. He was convinced that the only way he could keep the edge after a couple of all nighters', was to get "tossed" (my word for Meth-heads). After seeing my brother and Ben tweaked out of their minds and up for five days. I told them they looked like a tornado had come through, picked them up, and "tossed" them about 100 yards.

Soon after arriving at Ben's apartment in Joplin, I realized he was completely out of his mind. It took me half an hour to convince him I wasn't the Easter bunny, there to kill him with my big floppy ears. It took an hour, before he gave me the only information that didn't seem like incoherent garbage. "Anthony Stone," he cried out. "He . . .

he's going to kill me! I know it! Just like Eddie." He shortly thereafter, began to get frightened and was now cowering to the floor to crawl under the table. As I walked out the door, I grabbed Ben's address book, which was sitting on his kitchen table. Names, addresses, and phone numbers to everyone Ben knew or had known. I didn't think he would need it anymore.

That day was supposed to be my day of reckoning. I had finally tracked down the killer of my brother. As I pulled up across the street from where Anthony lived, I could have easily killed him there in the streets of Joplin. No one would have ever known it was me. And I could have been out of town before anyone had even noticed he was dead. But instead, my obsessive compulsive nature pushed me to ask the ultimate question, "WHY?" What could have been more important than the life of my brother?

I followed Anthony to a nearby club, where Anthony met up with his oldest friend, Justin. As they spoke together, I tried my best to make out what they were saying from across the room. But with people continually passing in front of me, I could not. Just as I was about to give up and try to move closer, I saw Justin mouth the words, "Phillip 66." I quickly escaped the mindless zombie rave and headed towards my car. I had just figured out what I needed to do. My way in through the doors of their membership only club, was in close range. But the only way the doors will open is by gaining their trust and confidence. Which was luckily headed my way in the form of a robbery.

I followed Anthony down the street to the convenient store. And as Anthony walked to the back of the store, I waited to make my move. I had the fore sight of what was to come and Anthony was about to be caught robbing the store. It was going to be pretty simple to keep him from getting caught. The officer that was supposed to arrest him was a loner. He didn't want anyone else to take credit for his busts nor did he see the relevance for a partner. So instead of calling for back up when he saw Anthony crawling out of the back window of the store. He just waited for Anthony to turn around and then yelled, "FREEZE!" Mistakes like these are common knowledge. This single mishap would not only send this police officer back to traffic duty but also leave him with a nasty headache when he wakes up.

I quietly stepped out of my car and slowly stepped up behind the officer. With a stick in my hand I crept closer and closer, until, "WHACK!" I motioned to Anthony, to get in the car, but he denied. I tried to tell him he didn't have enough time to get away by running. As the words slipped out of my mouth, we both heard sirens going off in the distance.

"Ok," Mrs. Maples interrupted as she crept out of the shadows of the room. "That's enough for today. We'll pick up where we left off next Sunday."

"So, Will," Elizabeth said as I grabbed my things, "I'm going to . . ."

"I would love to go with you to the beach next Sunday," I replied. She got confused and then quickly smiled a little as she finally remembered my psychic abilities.

Chapter 8

I secluded myself that Wednesday afternoon. I was sitting in the diner where Elizabeth and Lynn usually ate lunch. I was hoping that I would run into Elizabeth. Just so I would have an excuse to talk to her again. Over the last few months, it had seemed that I had forgotten what it was like to hold a decent conversation with someone. It could have also been that no one else had ever really taken an interest in me. I never was much of a "people" person. Not that I really prided myself on trying to be either. But my door to a normal life was closing fast. I needed to figure out which direction I was going to head and quick. I had a chance to go either way, obviously you can only pick one and both doors won't stay open forever, and you can't live on both sides of the line. It only becomes a lose-lose situation. I lose the opportunity at a normal life or my connection to my revenge.

My wish of a quiet lunch with Elizabeth was short lived, as David ran into the diner. Just by seeing his face, I knew today was going to be another one of those days. Not really a bad day, but not really a good day either. He began rambling about some guy wanting to kill him over a bad batch. I don't have the slightest idea of how any of that is David's fault; but the man was pretty adamant about it being David's problem. What most people don't understand is all we are basically doing is delivering the package. Most of the time we don't know what's in it, and if you don't like it, then buy from someone else. Don't get me wrong, we want the best product possible. But you're not going to get the best of the best, 100% of the time. Sometimes all you can get is mediocrity at best. It's not like we're trying to push toilet water splashed with a

41

little baking soda for our own amusement. It just so happens that is all we have at the time you need a fix.

"I need your help!" David said breaking my train of thought.

"What's new?" I replied shaking the cobwebs loose from the incoherent conversation I was having with myself.

I had just realized that I was about to skip school, again. I had planned on spending the lunch hour with the one person on the face of the planet that didn't seem to tick me off. But instead, I was going to head downtown, with someone who liked to push my buttons.

"Hey Will," Elizabeth said as she walked in with Lynn just behind her.

"Sorry, I have to take off," I replied. "David needs my help with something real quick. I should be back for class."

"Oh, ok," Elizabeth replied with an insecure look. I hated to see the disappointment in Elizabeth's eyes, but helping David was something I had to do. Not because I wanted to. But, because at some point in time; I would need his help in return.

"No, he doesn't!" Lynn said as she shot David an angered look. "He's not going anywhere!"

"There's that obsessive compulsive spirit I knew she was hiding," I said to myself. The soft spoken but to the point young lady I had met on my first day at the church, had somehow vanished. The woman that stood before me had transformed into an overprotective control freak. In reality who could blame her. We were about to skip school to go take care of a drug deal gone bad.

"No, I really do have to go, sorry babe," he said as he gave her a kiss and rushed me out the door. David knew better than to stay and fight with her. All she would have to say is, "I don't want you to go." And he would have stayed. But David could not take the chance. He needed to handle his business. I can't say that I wouldn't have done the same.

I didn't have the slightest idea of how I was going to get David out of his predicament. But I knew I would have to think of something soon. As we made our way downtown I began scanning my mind looking for a solution but came up with nothing. It was like God had showed me more than I should have seen the last time I helped David. God had figured out that if I had the chance to do something wrong, I would probably take the opportunity. This time he must have wanted me to handle it myself. I guess to test me. To see what I was made of.

I was still thinking about what to do when we pulled in the drive way. I should have never left the diner. I should have told David to call Sean or Steve and had my lunch with Elizabeth. But yet again, I am an idiot. Getting revenge had become like a drug to me. I needed my fix, for my addiction would not allow me to rest.

"This sucked!" I heard coming from the house as we walked up to the door. I rang the door bell and waited for a moment. I immediately heard a hushed scuffle in the house, "Shh . . ." A voice said, "It's the cops, I know it."

"Sam," David belted out, "open up, its David."

"Oh . . ." Sam said as he opened the door, "I hope you brought my money back."

I walked into, what I had assumed was the living room. The inhalation of nearby odors from un-bathed flesh and dog feces nearly swept me off my feet. There were news papers covering the entire floor; I am guessing, for when the dog relieved himself; all they had to do was pick up the paper and throw it away. There was a poker table in the center of the room, surrounded by two couches and a chair. In the corner, next to the front door was a small 13" television, tuned to the local cable channel. They were watching the greyhound races, which were taking place just outside of town.

"Last race of the day, put your money down," one of the men said.

"David," Sam said, "This was your best stuff? I wouldn't give this to my dog . . ."

"Ok," I interrupted. "Just give what you have left, back to me, and I'll fully reimburse you."

"Ah . . ." he stuttered for a moment.

"It's ok you can speak in full sentences, I do understand those," I said mocking him. "Wait," I laughed. "You finished off all three grams and you still want me to give you the money?!?" The man just stood there for a moment, thinking about what to say. I honestly thought the man was deranged or even mentally handicapped at least. Who in their right mind would think they would get money back, without the rest of the product? Leave it to an addict to believe they can get something for nothing in return.

As I began to become impatient with the man, he did the last thing I expected. "Yea, I do!" he said as he pulled out a butcher knife.

"You're kidding me, right!" I said as I began to laugh a little more at the man. "I'm going to give you a piece of information that is vital to your survival. The number starts at 25; the amount of time, in minutes, that I am spending away from a lunch with a beautiful woman. Next is 10; the amount of hours I have slept in the last week, and mind you, this is without a helping hand from some sort of drug. Then there is 6'9" and 320; the height and weight of the last man that pulled a knife on me. 8 feet; is where the man resides today, under a small slab of concrete I poured for my new basketball court. And last but not least, 2.1; the amount of seconds it will take for me to pull the gun from my waist and shoot you in the head. Now why don't you go ahead and let that linger in your melon for a few seconds before you make your move." Truthfully, I was bluffing. Killing is not really my forte. I will beat you up and take your shoes. But killing is more like a last resort, especially in this situation. I didn't even have a gun, but he didn't know that. I was just doing exactly what my brother had taught me, act as if. Act as if you are the meanest person alive. It works most of the time.

"Easy Will," David interrupted stepping in between us. "There's no reason we can't handle this like gentlemen."

I shook my head in disbelief of the man's ignorance and began to try and calm myself. I began to think of Eddie and what he would do in the situation. As I slowed my breathing down, I heard the TV naming the greyhounds for the last race of the day. "tsi-li-hu yo-na," (which is pronounced, chee-lee-who yoh-nuh.). The name caught me by surprise. I didn't understand why anyone would name their dog that, but who was I to judge. It was Cherokee, it meant, "sleeping bear." Coming from Oklahoma, you had to know at least a little Cherokee, or some other Native American language. At least 90 percent of my old high school was either, Native American or related by marriage to someone who spoke a Native American language. Eddie and I were lucky, our grandfather was half Cherokee. Every morning, he would wake Eddie and me up, by saying, "you sleep too much longer, and it's considered hibernation." He would follow it up by calling us, "tsi-li-hu yo-na."

"How about we make a bet?" I snapped back into the conversation.

"On what," Sam replied.

"The greyhound race," I answered, "If I win, I owe you nothing. And if you win, I'll give you your money back."

"Deal," Sam said, "pick your poison."

"tsi-li-hu yo-na, number 3," I answered. "And to make it easier for you, you can take the field."

It seemed like the race was over in a couple of seconds. Tsi-li-hu yo-na took off in the lead and never looked back. I didn't know for sure if he was going to win or lose but it was a gut decision, I am glad I made. Instead of getting into a fight with them, I seemed to use my mind, much like Eddie would have. In the long run it made things easier for everyone.

"Hey, Will," David said as we made our way out of the house and towards the vehicle. "How did you know who the winner was going to be . . ." He stopped for a second as he realized that I wasn't going to tell him. "You know at some point, you will have to tell me your secret of how you do that?"

"That's why it's called a secret David because I never tell anyone."

"Oh yeah," David said as he jumped in the truck. "Anyway, Matt wants you to meet up with him tonight."

I met Matt at the convenient store at the beginning of the beach access road. He only spoke to me for a matter of minutes as he watched me try his newest product. It was a drug dealer's code. Test the new guy with drugs and if he hesitates, he's not trustworthy. I had to go through the same thing with Anthony and Justin. I hate drugs. Along with my question of "why they killed my brother?" Drugs were the reason I let things with Anthony and Justin linger for too long. First I gained their respect by helping with a few problem areas. Then I gained their trust through loyalty and vigilance. The only thing I didn't plan on was becoming an addict. I lost focus and a piece of who I was in every pipe, syringe, and opened container. Until I woke up in jail two months' later, fighting conniptions, arguing semantics about religion with criminals, and an unrecognizable reflection.

"Thas a good dog," Matt said as he indulged my apprehensive obsession.

I sparked the lighter and begin heating the bulb, slowly twisting it and watching the crystals melt keeping the flame at a distance so that I would only slightly boil the contents instead of burning them up. I put my mouth to the opened end and began to inhale. A fog of poisonous inhabitations swept my thoughts as my lungs filled with toxic vapors. Heightened senses emerge from my depths, bringing with it, unassertive emotional baggage. Now struck with fear, my mind riddled with complexities foraging new tasteless outcomes from the loneliness of a self loathing life. Along with an empty soullessness that had been formed from a conquering low self esteem. All the while my mentality is weakened even more with every hit I take. Confined to my own memory, my reflection in the passenger side window is captured for evidential twinge, as an inexorable salty fluid thinly streamed down my right cheek. I quickly wiped the tear from my face as Matt continued his banter.

"What do you want from me?" I said hoping to stop his teases. He was so tweaked out of his mind, he could barely concentrate. He stumbled around it for a minute but finally asked if I would ride around with David permanently. Just in case there was something David could not handle. I guess so he would no longer need to bother Sean or Steve. I needed a moment to collect myself and found solitude in my own mind as I clarified my actions. *"Finishing what you started is vital to allowing yourself to move on. Only a few more weeks,"* I told myself.

"Friay Ny . . . meet me here at thish adresh," Matt ventriloquistly stammered. "We're havin' a pardie.

Chapter 9

After my brain had finished downloading the images from my dream, I rolled out of bed and began to get ready for school. In the other room I could faintly hear my father yelling into the phone receiver. "Oh great, he's in a bad mood!" I whispered to myself. I hurried along in hopes that he would not change the direction of his yelling. As I walked out of my room, he looked like he was still angry but had finally stopped yelling.

"Ok, whatever! I don't even care anymore!" He said sternly as he hung up the phone. I had a strange feeling that the other person on the line was my mother. I had only seen my father this angry twice. The first time was when I was ten years old. He told me I couldn't go to science camp because it was sacrilegious. In return for his honesty, I drove his brand new truck down the holler and into a pond. The only other time he was this angry, was when my mother told him she wanted a divorce. I haven't driven his truck in about a month, so it had to be something my mother said.

"Good morning pops," I said in a positive tone. I quickly sat down at the table and picked up the newspaper. Whether he was angry, sad, happy, or pleasantly comfortable his mood never mattered; my father always acted the same way regardless of the situation. You spoke to him in a positive tone and answer him with yes sir and no sir, or he will make you wish you were never born. He is much like a caged animal. He can be playful and seem like he is well adjusted. On the other hand, given the chance to pounce; he will eat your soul for lunch.

"I thought things were going to be different here?" He said as he turned his attention towards me.

This was another one of those my business is my business situations. But to make matters worse, I didn't have the slightest idea of what he was talking about. When you don't know what the other person is talking about, who in their right mind would give themselves up? I didn't know what to do so I continued on with my morning ritual of reading the newspaper. I quickly checked the date on the paper to make sure it was not from the day before. *"Nope,"* I said to myself as I read the date. My father liked to get the paper a day late, because in his own words, "Why should you have to pay for the paper? When you can get it for free a day later?" My father must be some sort of mastermind genius to come up with something that stupid.

"Hey, check it out!" I said as I read the headline on the front page, "Shootout gone right." I sat there reading the story aloud, when it finally struck me. The story I was reading, was about David and I. It was from the shootout we had downtown, when I shot the man in the hand. After the police arrived at the house they busted the two men. They were charged for a stolen car found in the garage, possession of narcotics, and a woman that had been kidnapped. She had been gagged and tied up in the basement. I kind of knew that they would be arrested, but their charges caught me off guard. Don't get me wrong, they got what they deserved but it was a little harsh for us to give them up for not giving us a few hundred dollars.

"Quit changing the subject," my father said still sounding a little agitated.

"Sorry," I replied, "What are you talking about?"

"You skipped school!" he snapped at me. "I thought we were going to start a new life and you were going to stay out of trouble?"

Like I said before, there was only one logical direction that would continue to calm him down. Instead of fighting with him, I replied, "sorry, it won't happen again, I promise."

"Your promises mean nothing here boy," he said as he took a deep breath in order to calm down. Just as I had presumed, the bomb was beginning to defuse. "Just stop getting into trouble . . ."

He could have said anything he wanted to after that, I had already fazed him out. I was already thinking about Sunday. I had planned to spend the day with Elizabeth and all I had to do was make it through school today. *"How hard could it really be?"* I thought to myself.

"No more trouble, alright?" My father said as he cradled his head in his hands.

"Yes sir," I answered.

Later that morning, when I made it to school, it seemed like David was waiting on me in the parking lot. He looked a little disturbed, at least a bit more than usual. He asked me if I saw the newspaper. As paranoid thoughts began rushing through his mind, I began to try and calm his fears. "What if the cops find out?" He snapped at me.

"What if they find out what, exactly? That we made their jobs easier for them?" I answered as we headed into the building. It's not like the two men were going to snitch on us. Even if they did, it's not like the police would believe them anyway. Why would any police officer take the word of a drug addict to heart and believe it to be factual.

"It's just a little too much for me. I think it's time . . ."

I knew that I was losing him and I needed to think of something quick before he decided to quit working for Matt. As I began to answer him, something caught my attention out of the corner of my eye. It was Elizabeth. She was talking to Luke. I didn't really know all that much about Luke other than he was a jock. He seemed like a decent person but I have been wrong before. I say this because I began to notice that Elizabeth was looking a little afraid of the situation. "We'll talk about this later," I said to David as I made a bee line towards Luke and Elizabeth.

"Look its simple, captain of the football team, head cheerleader," Luke said. "Now go out with me tonight," he continued with a smug look on his face.

This could be the answer to all of my problems. If she said yes, I would become a guy who is a friend, instead of the boyfriend. Not that I wouldn't want to be with her. She is exactly what I would look for in a partner. Our timing was just off a bit. All I had to do was just hope she said yes. *"Luke's demeanor was nice. He had a decent approach. Now let's see if he can stick the landing,"* I mocked him in my head.

"I said no, now leave me alone," Elizabeth answered. *"Ladies and Gentlemen,"* I continued in my mind to make fun of the situation. *"Luke has now fallen and tumbled off the mat completely and headed for the judges table face first."* It was all fun and games until she began to walk away. He stopped her by grabbing her by the shoulder and spinning her back around.

"I won't take no, for an answer," He replied.

Now I understand that women can take care of themselves. I am completely pro-feminism. "I can do everything you can do," none of that crap really means anything to me. But there are not too many things on the face of this planet that will tick me off faster than a man laying a hand on a woman. Be it a slap, a punch, or even a kiss. If they do not want to be touched, than you by God better not do it in front of me. "What part of no means no, do you not understand? I mean do you really think that's going to work?" I interrupted now stepping in between the two of them. "You know, you trying to pressure her into something she doesn't want to do."

"This is none of your business," He snapped at me.

"Don't do this Will," Elizabeth pleaded.

"Come on Eliza, just say yes," Luke said as he looked back at her.

"Oh, nice strategy, idiot" I laughed. "If all else fails, try the same thing again."

"Dude, I'm this close . . ." He said. He then flipped his hand up and showed me a small gap in between his fingers.

"Oh, I know this one. What is the real size of your brain?" I answered as he looked at me strangely. "We're playing a game, right!" I said as he turned quiet. "You know, you say something, and then I have to answer it with a question." I could almost sense the blood beginning to boil in his body. It wouldn't be long before he took a swing at me. I was trying to contain myself, but I just couldn't do it. "My turn," I said, "I'm a moron, who thinks he's the greatest person of all time. But in reality, in two years, I'll live in a single wide trailer. I will spend my days thinking about the glory days, while'st in a drunken rage or at my job. The same job in which I wear overall's, with the name tag sewn in them. So people everywhere will know the name of the guy who pumps their gas."

"Will!" Elizabeth said trying to stop me.

"No, I'm sorry Elizabeth," I answered. "The answer was Luke."

"Please stop," she said. With her voice a little shaky, she began to move around beside me. I didn't want to take my eyes off of Luke, but I needed to move her out of harm's way. She was standing too close. So I began to nudge her out of the way. As I began to move her back, my eyes locked onto hers, and I felt a chill causing me to pause my motion. I instantly remembered my father's words from earlier that morning, *"just stop getting into trouble."* But I could no longer help myself. I had already sensed that it was too late. *"Oh well,"* I thought. *"At least I'll get to play my little game, of see if you can hit me, again."*

Something was off or different at least. Something just didn't feel right. It was almost like the painful fear I had felt while I was at Eddie's gravesite. I was terrified of what was to come. Not from the knockout punch I was about to receive from Luke, but the thereafter consequences of my actions. Would my wrong doings, cost me someone close to me. I don't remember much after that following thought. I had apparently thought for too long and Luke had tried his best to put his fist through my head. I couldn't believe that I had allowed that Neanderthal to hit me. But he did, right square in the jaw. As I slipped into unconsciousness, my dream from the church classroom began again.

I was in that same strange bed, when I heard that, now familiar scream. I again, rushed out the door, but this time I at least made it down the hallway. I ran up to the door from where the scream was coming from; and saw the same green construction paper I had seen many times before. When Eddie and I were still living at home, he had the same piece of paper on his door. It read, "Eddie's room. Keep out." As I opened the door, the light from inside seemed like it nearly blinded me. As my eyes came back into focus, I found myself lying down in the nurse's office of the high school.

I sat there for a moment, just trying to collect my thoughts and remember what happened. I couldn't understand why I kept having the same dream over and over again. Were the dreams visions of things to come? Or was I finally having real dreams again? If I was having real dreams again that could only mean one thing. God had finally withdrawn my abilities and was not allowing me to act in such an unscrupulous manner anymore. *"Thank God,"* I thought. I never wanted these gifts in the first place. These burden riddled gifts, were nothing more than a way for God to delegate power. Heaven forbid that God should actually have to take care of his/her own problems. But there was only one question that I really wanted to be answered. What was in the room that was so important?

"You didn't have to do that," Elizabeth said as she saw my eyes open.

"No, I'm fine. Thanks for asking," I fired back.

"Sorry," she sighed. "Are you ok?"

"I'll live! How's Luke's fist?" I continued jokingly. "I think he might have cut his knuckle on my tooth."

"This isn't a joke!" She said as a tear streamed down her face.

I had never seen someone get so worked up over a fight. It wasn't even a real fight. "Come on don't do this! Quit being so sensitive! It was one punch!"

"I just hate fighting. There's no sense in it."

"Look, I wasn't even going to do anything. I was fine, sitting on the sidelines, until he put his hands on you. I'm sorry, but that's crossing the line. The gloves come off. I just can't control myself when something like that happens."

"Yes, I understand that. But, why does everything have to turn into violence with you?"

"Good question," I said to myself. It's been twenty minutes since Elizabeth left the room and I'm still bewildered from the question. It seemed that I usually had all the right answers but I couldn't stop thinking, *"why did I always turn to violence? What was I trying to prove? That I was the toughest and smartest person in school? Who really cares about that crap anyway?"* It was the first time, at least since Eddie had passed, in which I had someone leave me speechless. I hated being wrong, but I had to admit, I had a distinct feeling that I was. *"I could have asked him politely to keep his hands off of her. I could have been direct with my feelings. I could have also sat around in a powwow with the two of them and talked about how different things made us feel. And ask them what color I needed to paint my nails, to go along with the dress I was going to wear that night as well. Not even an inkling of any of that seemed even close to my style. I am a living, eating, breathing man. I shouldn't feel the need to apologize, for something I believed was the right thing to do."* At least I thought so.

After getting home, it didn't take long for my father to figure out what had happened. All it took was one look at my jaw and my father began to lay down the law. As if he really knew what was best for me. He was more of a pretend father figure. When I needed him, he was never there. And when I didn't, I couldn't get rid of him. My father always seemed like a greener pastures kind of guy. Even with our family, other than Eddie, he always seemed like he thought he deserved better.

"I fell down," I said hoping he would buy it.

"The school called!" He replied angrily as I sighed. "Maybe you should think about . . ."

I could have listened to the outlandish things my father had conjured up to let me know that I was a bad child. But I was busy thinking about spending the day with Elizabeth on Sunday. We apparently had things we needed to talk about. I fazed him out as best as I could, and continued on my quest to answer a few of my questions from earlier that day.

First, why did I always turn to violence? I didn't really know why, but it could be an easy fix. I had seen Eddie out smart people before. He would begin with something small and before long they would notice even their friends were laughing at them. Sometimes, Eddie could get a little harsh with the things he said and I would almost feel sorry for the person. My second question rolling around in my head, was why had I gotten hit in the first place? Maybe God was trying to show me that even if I saw everything before it happened, that he wasn't going to let me win every battle. I didn't think that he/she was going to allow me to do whatever I wanted, whenever I wanted.

". . . and that's why you're grounded for a week!" My father yelled as I finally started to pay attention to the conversation again.

"But!" I started.

"No Buts'," he barked. "Now, go to your room!"

"Whatever," I sighed as I headed to my room.

"There will be no cursing in my house!"

"I said, 'Whatever' you pompous, arrogant . . ."

"Make it two weeks for that last statement," my father said as he began to feel good about how he had handled the problem.

"Who gives a crap!?!" I yelled as I slammed the door shut. I had many things running through my mind that day, but it had seemed that my father could care less. I realize that I didn't even try to explain it to him, but I myself couldn't understand my own thoughts. How could I even begin to translate what had happened, if I couldn't find the words to explain it to myself? I just chalked the argument up to, my father didn't understand me, and that he was a narcissist. It was like he only cared about himself. As if he were too busy to care about anything that might happen to anyone else.

At least my fights with my father were beginning to mellow out a bit. With my psychic like abilities, it has been a matter of months since I have sensed his true hatred for me. Although tonight was not one of those nights, on occasion, I can almost sense the words coming out of my father's mouth. He would never actually say them, but I can hear them nonetheless. As insensitivity and rage infiltrates his mentality, his mind wonders towards the same words, "The wrong one died. The wrong son lost his life. Why couldn't it have been you?" And as much as it kills me inside to hear these types of things, he is absolutely right. I mean, I get it. I understand his anguish. I miss Eddie every day of my life and I'll probably feel this way for the remainder of my existence. The better son did die a few months ago. And if I were given the opportunity to make things right, I would gladly lay down my own life for his. Eddie deserved better. Both of them deserved better. *"But the past is history, and the future has potential, but the present is now. And right now, I need to get to a party,"* I thought to myself.

After locking the door to my bedroom, I quietly opened the window, and removed the screen. As I slipped out the window, I had a strange feeling that something bad was about to happen. *"I could have really used your help today Eddie. I wish you were here,"* I told myself as I pushed my truck down the driveway. It had seemed that things were beginning to fall apart.

Chapter 10

As I pulled down the street where the party was taking place, I noticed the festivities were much larger than I had assumed. The front yard and the streets surrounding the house were completely flooded with vehicles from fellow partiers. I had to park over a block away and it seemed like everyone from the school had shown up. I made my way up the street and then through the yard. I cut in between vehicles and even had to weave, duck, and dodge through a few people just to get around to the front door.

"Will!!! Jus tha persin I wannid ta see!" Matt said as he stepped out the front door. "I god a surprise fur ya."

As we walked into the house, Matt began talking about something that David had done. I couldn't quite make out exactly what he was talking about, but I tried my best to keep up. Apparently, David had come by and was explaining to Matt why he could no longer work for him. Meanwhile as their argument commenced, Lynn sat in David's truck waiting on him. Before long she began to get agitated and decided to go see what was taking so long. When she couldn't find David, she began to drink and started partying with everyone else. As Matt began to see Lynn letting loose, he began to mellow out a bit. By then she was already drunk and stumbling everywhere. So he sent David to get some more ice and convinced him that Lynn would be fine until he got back.

"Ya don walk away from ush, we walk away from you," he said. As he opened the door to the guest room of the house, I peered into darkness. It took a moment for my eye's to focus in the dark, but things were beginning to clear up a little. It was Steve. He was leaning over the top of some girl. He was undoing her blouse, and kissing her neck. "You nex?" He asked. "She wone even know tha we're doin' anythin', she's pasd owt."

As my eyes began to adjust a little more in the dark I could almost make out what her face looked like. "Who is it?" I asked.

"Thas his girlfriend." Matt answered.

"I already had this fight once today," I thought to myself. My mind instantly went blank as I rushed through the door towards Steve. In my moment of no turning back (and by "no turning back" I mean as my body flying through the air.), my mind then wondered to my new complexities. I had started to do drugs again, which was a problem in its self. I was here to seek my revenge and now I had complicated things by making friends. I began to get angry as my fist collided with Steve's face. I felt no pain from the adrenaline pumping through my veins at an accelerated rate but I felt a sense of relief for I was finally doing something right. After finally getting back to my feet, I had noticed that Lynn had been somehow startled awake.

"What's going on?" She asked.

"It's ok," I said trying to calm her. *"What have I done? How could I have let this happen?"* I thought as I began to wrap her in the blanket. I knew at the time that it was not completely my fault, but I still had a hand in her misfortune. I know that I could have done something different. My mission in life was beginning to have casualties that never deserved my problems. "I'll get you out of here. I promise. Nothing's going to happen to you."

"Wod are ya doin'?" Matt yelled.

The light coming from the hallway behind me, fluttered a bit as he began to charge at me. As I turned around, he stopped in his tracks, and threw a wild left jab. Foresight into his actions was detrimental, for I knew what it would take for Lynn and me to get away. Knocking him out was completely out of the question. Striking a crack head unconscious is nearly impossible to do with the use of a baseball bat. So I quickly grabbed his wrist with my left hand and with an open palm struck his elbow with my right. "CRACK!" I had never heard a bone break that loudly before. It was an absolutely disturbing sound that, to be completely honest, was a little sickening. You know that feeling when your stomach kind of flips and leaves a bad taste in your mouth. That's what just happened.

"Argg!!!" Matt yelled. "This ain over Will!" He cried out.

I turned around, reached down, and picked Lynn up in my arms. I didn't really know exactly what to do, but I quickly made my way down the hall towards the front door. I rushed out into the crowded front lawn and eventually out to my truck. It was strange. With my habitual endless moments that I spend, thinking about what to do all the times; at any given moment, was beginning to diminish. For once I wasn't just thinking about myself.

As I sat Lynn down in the seat, I heard a voice come from behind me. "Will!"

"Do we really have to do this, again? You know it's only going to end, with me making you look like a fool, again," I said as I turned around.

"Well," Sean answered. "I know what you did and it was for good reason. At least make it look like I tried to stop you."

"Thanks Sean," I said with a smile.

"No," he stopped me. "Thank you. For not making me, be the one to put an end to it." I didn't even have to think about it twice. I doubled up my fist and struck him across the jaw. The giant ape took a moment, shook his head, and stumbled a little bit. He gave a quick grin and then fell to the ground. In a different situation, I would have stayed to laugh at him when he awoke. But needless to say, this wasn't the time.

"Would you like me to take you to the police station or something?" I asked as we headed down the road.

"Why?" She questioned. "To go to the police station I would need some sort of evidence of the crime. There is no proof of any sort, no bruising, no DNA, and there is only hearsay of testimonials from the two of us. This in return would be put into question because there would be two others opposing our statements with their own morbid recollection. With the way the judicial system is set up. I would most likely spend months and maybe even years, through a trial of speculation; divulging into the worst night of my life; reliving every moment as if it were happening all over again, only to watch my attacker walk away unscathed from a lack of corroboration. I don't think so. You can take

57

me home. I believe they got what they deserved by your hands anyway. If you feel the need to do me any favors, just don't tell David what happened. A matter of fact, don't tell anyone. Promise me."

"I promise," I answered. "I won't tell anyone."

It's hard to dispute the truth, so I did not. Logic was definitely something she did not lack. It was nice change to see someone else take control of a situation. She wouldn't allow even one aspect of what had happened to break her. I couldn't help myself but to admire her. She had just gone through something so detrimental it would cause most women to shell up. Most women would begin to lash out at any man who even stepped near them. But her obsessive controlling mind, wouldn't allow her to conduct herself in such a manner.

I felt the need to tell her something. Her bravery deserved something along the lines of a life changing event. As I thought of what to tell her, I blurted, "Caterpillar." As I read her movements and oncoming questions, I planned for her rebuttal. The one thing I didn't plan for was the reasoning behind the word. Caterpillar wasn't just an argument over Halloween costumes with her mother. It was also her nickname. *"Tears could start flowing any minute now. Get a hold of the situation now, before it gets out of hand,"* I said to myself. "My brother passed away a few months ago, his nickname for me was little bro'," I told her. "He wasn't the greatest person on the face of the planet but he wasn't the worst either. And what's worse is that I was given these psychic abilities. Abilities that allow me to see the present, past, and future, but they weren't enough to allow me to save my brother. Every once in a while I can hear him talk to me, almost like he's guiding me. And I can hear other voices as well. I guess people trying to reach out, hoping to help their family members to move on without them."

"What are you getting at?" She asked as she tried to contain herself.

"Look, you don't have to believe me when I say that I have spoken with your mother. And you don't have to believe that she said she loves you and is proud of you. But on the other hand, how else would I know that your nickname since infancy was Caterpillar?" I stopped for a moment allowing everything to sink in. "We have the same situation in both of our lives with completely different circumstances. I'm a hermit.

I despise everything about myself and I hate every second I wasted not being around my brother more often. But you on the other hand have allowed yourself to have a life. You have a family that loves you, a significant other that would do anything for you, and to be completely honest I'm envious. You inspire me to want more out of my life, and for that, I thank you."

It took a couple of minutes for her to find the words, but my affect on her led her to say, "You're welcome."

"Ok, you're home," I said. "Would you like me to walk you to the door?"

"If it's not too much to ask," she replied.

"It's not," I answered. After getting out of my truck, I walked around to open her door, and began trying to explain. "I hope you know that nothing actually happened back there . . ."

"Weren't you scared back there?" She stopped me as we began to walk up the sidewalk.

"Only a fool would say no," I answered. "I respect all of Gods creations, but I fear nothing of this earth. What I dreaded was not what you thought was scary. I was concerned that if the girl in the room wasn't you. Would I have still done what I did?"

"I believe you would have," she said. Again she stood before me. And again she didn't allow herself to feel the twinge of shame upon humanity for her night of discomfort; nor exasperation that would be followed shortly by the unavoidable sobs of the mentally broken. In surprising fashion, she not only recognized the situation, but tried to make me feel better about the result. Her selflessness was a commendable trait one could only hope to emulate. Only a week and a half ago, I had assumed that her controlling spirit was nothing more than a character flaw. It turns out that it was actually a noble strength.

"Lynn! Where have you been?" Elizabeth asked as she opened the door. "Oh my god, what happened?!?"

"She'll be fine," I replied. "She just needs to sleep it off."

"I'm not speaking to you, brute!" Elizabeth said as she slammed the door in my face.

"How can she still be mad at me?" I thought to myself as I headed home. But she had a point. I was acting a bit barbaric with the way I

handled things earlier that day. I couldn't be mad at her for telling the truth. She was only making an observation or best educated guess from my reactions. Was it her fault that I was acting like a simpleton? Was it her fault I got carried away? As much as I wanted to think it out more thoroughly, I became distracted. I now had a new question lingering in my mind. I had lied to Lynn tonight and I didn't lose my abilities in the process. I mean, I can't speak to the dead. I don't even know where I come up with the idea; nor did I have any idea of how it would even be possible.

As I pulled into the driveway of my house, I saw that the light to the living room was still on. I stepped out of the truck, slowly closed the door, and began to sneak around the corner of the house. I instantly felt like I was a secret agent sneaking around stealing secrets from other countries. But come to find out, I was more like an assailant from one of those police videos. I was about to be caught red handed, doing something completely idiotic.

I slipped my fingers underneath my slightly cracked window, and little by little, inched the window open. I slipped one foot in through the open space and began to heave myself in through the opening in my room. As I lost my footing, because I was standing on a barbell, I slipped and fell towards the ground. In mid air as if I had forgotten to not make any noise, I flipped around to catch myself with my hands. As I hit the floor it looked more like I was doing a push up as I slowed myself. "Agility like a cat," I told myself. Letting out a sigh of relief, I then rolled over to my back, and bumped into the table next to my bed with my shoulder. The table didn't make much noise, but the lamp on top of it began to tumble to the floor towards my head. Needless to say, catching the lamp in my hands in what seemed like a pitch black room. Was much harder than I had assumed, but I caught the lamp nonetheless. The only problem was that it was a touch lamp. Any time anyone touched it with even just a finger, it would light up. It had three settings bright, medium, and dim. As soon as the lamp hit my hands I quickly tapped it three more times to turn it off. Again, there was no noise made. And I seemed to get the lamp turned off in enough time before my father, sitting in the living room, noticed. I placed the lamp back on the table and stood up in the again drastically darkened room.

I then made my way to my dresser. After donning on some lighter clothing and stepping out to use the restroom, my father caught me at the bathroom door.

"William Joseph Larson," my father sternly barked down the hallway. "I need to speak with you for a moment."

I didn't know exactly what the problem was, but the three name beckon meant it was something severe. That is a child's signal to let them know that someone has done something sincerely wrong. "Ah, yes sir," I answered as I headed down the hallway to the living area.

"Is there anything you want to tell me?" He asked as I sat down on the couch.

"I don't know what did you hear?" I said trying to lighten the mood.

"Fine," my father said as he leaned back in his chair. "Until you tell me the truth we will step up from the usual grounding to a reflective grounding."

In my family there were two types of groundings. The first consisted of only weekdays. You would go to school, come directly home afterwards, and spend the remainder of the day in your room. Of course that was until bedtime, when you got to go to sleep just to wake up, and start the whole process over again. Weekends were optional. Meaning it mattered what mood my father was in on Saturday and Sunday to be allotted a free pass for the day. The second was reflective grounding. The weekdays were spent exactly in the same manner, but weekends were spent a little differently. It was what Eddie and I considered being more like lock down in the prison system. We would spend all day Saturday and Sunday in our rooms, reflecting back to a time in our life when we had made a similar mistake. Later that night, usually after dinner, you would have about thirty minutes to plead your case. It took remembering at least three past transgressions, and more often than not; one heck of a conclusion, before our parents would let us off the hook.

"Come on Pops," I replied. "That's a little bit of an aggressive reaction, for me not even knowing what I did wrong."

"I'm sorry you feel that way, but you know the rules in my household. No bad deed goes unpunished," he answered. "You've done something wrong and you know it. You basically told on yourself by coming in here with your shirt inside out. You went out tonight and now you are trying to lie about it?"

"Pops," I began to interject. I had gone through all of the sneaking around; the unpleasantness of falling to my face; and almost having a lamp crush my face. There was no way I was going to spend all that time covering up the truth; just to let it all slip between the cracks because my father assumed something. He had no real proof. Maybe he walked into my room and I was not there. I could cover that up with being in the bathroom. Or he yelled for me and I did not answer. I could say that I stepped outside for some fresh air. I didn't go through all of that for nothing. I don't think so. My father will have to try much harder than that if he wanted to catch me. "Maybe I just felt like wearing the shirt inside out," I replied.

"Nice try," he barked. "Lynn called five minutes ago, to make sure you made it home safely."

"Son of a . . ." I sighed. I forgot to tell everyone else the situation.

"Tomorrow will be a reflective day," he said. "That should give you something to think about while you're trying to go to sleep. NOW GO TO BED!"

Chapter 11

"*O*ne full day of reflection," I thought to myself as I got out of bed. *"I need three life altering stories and a conclusion that will knock Pops off his feet."* I had one day to finish my verbal essay. Oh, how I loathed reflective groundings but I had no choice. At least it was only one day. After brushing my teeth and a shower, I headed towards the kitchen to get some breakfast. *"Might as well get the face to face altercation over with,"* I continued to reminisce in my mind. Obviously, it was going to be an awkward meal but best to just get it over with than dread the inevitable. As I walked down the hall something was different about the house. It was quiet. My father was gone. *"He must be going insane to think that I'm going to stay in the house, while he is off doing whatever he wants."*

As I made my way through the living room towards the kitchen, something caught my eye. There on the front door of the house was a handwritten note from my father. It read,

William,

I understand that we as a family are having some problems adjusting to a new life and I get that you need your own space. So if you don't feel that you need to do the day of reflection, that is fine, I do understand. I don't want to make you feel like you must do anything. In a few months you will be eighteen, and in within the next year, you will most likely be headed off for college. You are no longer the child I have been trying to protect for the last seventeen years *and at some point you will need to make your own decisions. I now give you the opportunity for one of the first of many decisions. If you don't spend the day in reflection, I will take it as you have decided to grow up and declared for some sort of emancipation from your mother and me. I would also like to point out that if you decide to leave the house at any time, I will assume you have decided to move out on your own. And if that happens, I would like to wish you the best of luck in your future endeavors. I will not lead you in the direction that I would like you to take and I cannot tell you what direction is best for you either. All I can really do is try to give you some advice. Before making a choice in what you should do, especially with it being your first major decision. You might want to think it out thoroughly, weighing out all of your options. And last but not least, when you make your decision, stick with it and push forward. No matter what you choose I hope you know that your mother and I love you dearly and only hope for the best for you. Good luck son.*

Dad

"Great a full day of reflection," I told to myself. I mean what was there to really think about? The decision was already made for me in his letter. My father may not seem like the smartest man in the world but he is deceptively intelligent. The letter could only have two meanings. The first is that he actually meant every word of it. The second is that it was some sort of bullying technique into seeing what I was made of mentally. I could either prove him right by staying in the house and doing exactly what he had asked me to do. Or move out and prove him right about me still being childish and not being able to stand on my own two feet. If I moved out, there is no way I could find an apartment in such a short time. And even if I did, I'm not old enough to sign a lease. Not only that but somehow I would have to find a good enough job to pay all of the rent and various other bills. So my choices really narrowed down to; either sleep in an alley on a cold slab of concrete or sleep in my own bed.

After admitting to myself that I literally had no other place to go, I ate my breakfast and headed back to my room. I collapsed on my bed and closed my eyes awaiting some sort of visual compass. I needed a direction for my conclusion of the stories. But instead of thinking of a direction, the first story crept up from my memory.

When Eddie and I were children we didn't have much family other than our parents. Like I said before, my father's side was filled with addicts. So spending any time with them was completely out of the question. On my mother's side there was a huge rift from my grandparent's divorce. And with my parent's being a passive couple, they felt it would be easier to not choose either side. Eddie tried to tell them that just because we went to see one side of the family. The other would not try to assume that we have chosen a side, and vice versa. But no matter what we said, it would not change their minds.

Anyway, the only things even remotely close to being a family to us was the church we went to. There were a few children close to our age, but I didn't really like them. I didn't really like anyone. Eddie was always more of the "people person." I just assumed those people were more of a waist of my time. I spend most of my time in my head, and I love every second of it. If I started to interact with other people, then they might assume we were friends, and try to speak to me every time we saw each other. Even just opening up to one person and holding a conversation, could be detrimental to my daydreamer status. All it would take is one person seeing me talk to someone else and that would open the door to them trying to talk to me as well. I mean, I now understand that communication with another person is vital to keeping a sane mind. But at the time, I would never allow anything like that to happen. Don't get me wrong, there were a plethora of conversations I would have loved to jump in on. But I believed my childhood was totally and completely a learning phase. You cannot jump into a conversation and say "I believe . . ." without knowing all of the facts in the scenario. "That would only make you look stupid," I would say trying to restrain myself. But behind these various conversations that I had the utmost admiration for and so desperately wanted to join, was another complex mind. Much like the minds that Eddie and I had. Her name was Teresa Sullivan.

Mrs. Sullivan wasn't a doctor; she wasn't a teacher, nor was she a college graduate. I don't even think she was a high school graduate. But she had an uncanny ability to say one thing and make everyone stop in their tracks to think about it for a moment. Her decisive intriguing mind captivated and enticed not only my devilishly clever mind, but Eddie's as well. The two of us spent as much time as we possibly could around her, and she continually gave us reasons to enjoy her company. It was not really a first crush type of moment because she was in her sixties. But more of a mental flexibility preparation moment, like the time Eddie and I went to her house to help her with her garden.

"Edward, William," Mrs. Sullivan said as she answered the door. "Perfect timing, follow me."

We followed her through her house into the back yard. Apparently we were going to plant some new flowers in her garden. It was kind of our little trade off. She would council, as we helped her with heavy lifting, and other various strenuous chores, such as: cleaning out the gutters, mowing the lawn, and even putting a new roof on her house last spring. On many occasions she finds our agreement to be a little one sided. So she tries to pay us from time to time. It's not a lot of money but she gives what she can. What she does not know is that she always gets the money back. Before we leave, we ask for something to drink. While she fetches the glass of water or tea, Eddie slips the money in a couch cushion or her coat pocket. We did the same type of things to our grandparents (when we saw them) and our parents.

"So where did we leave off last time?" She asked.

"We left off with forgiveness," Eddie answered.

"Oh, yes," she said as she handed us a shovel.

"You see, I find myself apologizing constantly," Eddie said. "I don't really know what for? But I have the distinct feeling that I'm not doing something right. For instance: I'm doing very well in school. I will eventually become the valedictorian. I've already scored a perfect score on my college aptitude test and I'm only a sophomore. In a few years I could head off to any university my heart desires. But that's not the direction I believe I am supposed to be going. It seems like everyone has such high hopes for me and they rely on me for many things. So I push in one direction and find myself turning around to ask for forgiveness because I have let someone down. On many occasions, I feel that everyone knows where my life is headed, except for me."

"No Edward," she stopped him. "The tulips go over here."

"Oh, sorry," he apologized.

"You are not forgiven," she answered as the both of us gave her a puzzled look. Now with an alluring congregation behind her she continued, "Just go with me on this Edward. How can you ask for forgiveness, when you don't know how to forgive?"

"What are you talking about? I forgive people all the time."

"I'm not talking about forgiving someone else. I'm sure you mean it every time you utter the words. I'm talking about learning how to forgive yourself," she answered. "Through selfless actions, you put yourself in harm's way. You pay mentally and physically, for more than just your own faults. You are trying to fill the void from the problems you have caused with trying to fix everyone else's. You may be able to fix all of your problems, just by understanding that mistakes are made on a daily basis and most of them cannot be avoided. When you do finally forgive yourself, I am sure that many things in your life will begin to change."

"Like what?" He asked.

"Well for instance: before you believed that you were the problem, and you might have been right; doubtful, but maybe. What you do not understand is that you may have been the problem, then. But now, you are the solution. Now you know what direction will lead you down a wrong path. You know what could cause someone else heartache and you refrain from it. The biggest helping hand you can give now is to that fifteen year old monk over there," she continued as she pointed me out. "His five year hiatus of uttering even a single word is his process of learning everything he can without getting in the way. He not only learns from his own mistakes but from yours as well. He can be a better person by watching or hearing the errors you have made in your lifetime. And even though he tries to stay out of everyone's way, and it may seem like he is, he himself is not mistake free."

"What makes you say that?" Eddie asked.

"Because he just crushed my petunias," she answered as we laughed.

Not only was it one of the most well thought out conversations I had ever been a part of; but it was also the last discussion we had with Mrs. Sullivan, for she died only a few of weeks later.

"I will never forget you Mrs. Sullivan," I thought as I welcomed myself back to reality. I opened my eyes and made my way towards the kitchen to get something to drink. As I passed by the front door, I again glimpsed at the letter. Not because there might have been something I had missed, but because it was more of an outline of what I really needed to think about. Eddie's approach to this type of punishment was to think of the good lessons he had learned in life. Thusly delegating him as the more affectionate one and making him stride to make more elated accomplishments in the future. When all I did was take a gloomy and negative course with the grasp of my own penalties. I had already decided quite a few times in the last couple of weeks. That Eddie's way of thinking would lead to much better circumstances. So I again would continue on with his type of superior excellence in doing what was right.

Chapter 12

As I made my way back to my room, I discovered the bearing I would need to take for the conclusion of my stories, family. It was an important lesson that my father thought I needed to learn. In times of great depression one always turns to family. When things overwhelm you into an almost vegetative state of mind, you turn to family. And when you desperately need something to keep you on the right track, you again, turn to family. My father's outline for discussion that he bestowed upon me, in letter form; was that if I took the time to look around, I no longer had any family, other than my mother and him. Apparently, it was an aspect of my life that he believed I needed to change.

As I fell to my bed, I immediately closed my eyes, and I again began thinking of more family lessons. The first thing that came to mind was the first miracle I had ever witnessed. It was vital to my family's survival, and from a religious stand point, it was essential to changing my own beliefs. And with the assumption that my father may feel a little left out, in my growing education of my fellow man. I decided it would be best if I included him in my next story.

At the time, nine years old, I had read various "history books" or what most people call "Bibles." And with deep regret from knowing what I know now, I assumed that there was no God, nor a son of God. I believed there was no God because of the destruction that mankind had made on a regular basis. And it seemed, at the time, there was no God to stop it from happening. My non belief in Jesus as the son of God, which is still a touchy subject in my household and a lingering question that many believe will never be answered. But he always seemed more like an over glorified saint. From what I have read and speculated about; is that he seemed more like an average man. A run of the mill guy with a back story filled with nothing more than rumors. For the longest time I presumed that Jesus' apostles, the evangelists of old, and even the leaders of various congregations that we have in today's world; were nothing more than political money hungry wolves feasting on our emotions and wallets. I mean, after hearing phrases like: "Do you feel the spirit of the lord working amongst us today?", "Can you feel the awesome power of the lord opening your heart?", and "can you sense the strength that God has given you?" Of course you believe you can feel the strength, power, or spirit of the lord almighty. Who would blame anyone for saying that they felt "something" after the 30-45 minute emotional slap in the face that they had just received.

I was emotionally hopeful to the possibility of there being a higher power, but pessimistic to the idea of it actually being factual. You see, that was my real problem, thought. I was definitely too smart for my own good. I looked at my religious surrounding community as nothing more than feeble minded drones. They read through their bibles or what I like to call "history books." And went from page to page saying, "If I do this God will punish me and turn me into a pillar of salt;" or "If I do this God will bless me with an abundance of crops;" I knew that I couldn't have been the only person thinking that it was a load of crap, but what would I know, I was just a kid.

Now with keeping all of that in mind, and knowing these were thoughts of a nine year old. I say again, with a deep regret from knowing what I know now. All of the unanswered questions surrounding God, Jesus, the Apostles, and even modern day evangelists; went right out the window when I witnessed my first of many miracles.

After leaving, yet another affectionate sermon from our local vulture in deacon clothing, I began my mental criticism of his message. Becoming deeply concerned with the direction of the conversation my parents were having in the front seat. I dove head over heels into their discussion. "What makes you think that he will actually do it?" I questioned.

"Because when this family is in need, we always have, and will continue to rely on God to provide for us. He is the reason we live and he will be the reason we survive," my father answered. My family had fallen on financial hard times. My father was laid off from his job almost a week ago and our electricity had already been shut off. "You do believe God will provide for us don't you?"

"Ah, sure," I lied.

My father recognized my hesitation and made a request, "Believing is a hard thing for a kid to grasp. So why don't we put it to a test?"

"Ok," I answered. I loved tests and it would most likely be a test to Gods power. I would finally find out the truth.

"Ok," my father continued. "Tonight I want you to pray for food and we'll see what happens."

"How is that a fare test? Everyone in the family can't pray for the same thing," I said.

"Ok," my father continued speaking to my mother and Eddie. "Nobody pray tonight. We will all rely on William and his prayers only."

There was actually a pretty good chance that this would be a great test. My family wasn't really the type of people to ask for help from the church or really anyone other than God. Nobody knew about our heartaches and need for supplies. It would just be me asking God to provide for us and awaiting his answer.

Nothing really out of the ordinary happened for the rest of that Sunday. Nobody told me what I needed to pray for. They didn't give me a list of items we needed. Nobody even reminded me that I needed to pray that night. Everyone just let it go as if they knew it would be taken care of properly.

That night, before I went to sleep, I knelt down in front of my bed and began my silent prayer. "Dear Lord," I began to ask. "If you do exist, you know that I don't do this very often. Usually when Eddie is praying, I drop to my knees, and make believe to pray because I never really believed in you. But as much as I would like to pretend that this and you are some sort of joke or prank. My family and I are in dire need of your guidance and some food. Truthfully you know that I deeply desire the ability to believe in you. I want that unflappable faith that you give my parents and Eddie on a daily basis. If proven right that you do exist, I submit myself as your servant. I will confide in you to lead me in the right directions from now on," I continued as an emotional chill crept up my spine giving me peace of mind and body. It felt like a monumental release from my worldly views and I cared for nothing more than the opportunity to breathe another breath. "With food in mind, I really don't know what to ask for. Maybe a couple of steaks or even just a few potatoes would be sufficient. I ask all of this in your name Lord. Amen."

After finishing my prayer, I hastily curled up on my bed before someone walked in on me with tears flowing from my eyes. I instantly buried my face in my pillow as an unrelenting emotional downpour flushed through every inch of my body. Was this happening because I had finally given my life to God? Was God going to answer my prayers? Or was this all a ploy from an over abundance of lectured garbage shoved down my throat? *"None of it matters,"* I told myself. *"My answers will be here tomorrow,"* I continued as I rolled over onto my side and allowed my mind to drift into darkness.

Awakened not from a nightmare but a cold sweat nonetheless, I grabbed my flashlight and looked at my watch. *"5:21 in the morning is a little early,"* I thought to myself. There was something happening. I didn't really know what, but I had one of those gut wrenching feelings like someone had died. Whatever it was, it was keeping me awake. I just stayed in my bed thinking of past discrepancies, present discoveries, and future devotions. One after another, thoughts began to voyage through my mind. What I would do in religious like settings? Would I continue making the right decisions? Was life as I knew it going to change? Where would I be in a couple of years? What was the divine reasoning behind humanity? In a matter of hours I went from having no faith in God to believing he existed and now to a distinct feeling that I knew he would provide for my family.

After about two hours of guess work on my livelihood, I was startled by a noise downstairs. I walked down the hallway, down the stairs, and into the seemingly empty living room. "God, is that you?" I asked.

"No, its Dad," my father answered.

"Sorry Pops," I replied. "I thought you were someone else."

"Ok," my father said as he laughed a little.

As I was about to begin telling my father what happened that night, we heard a loud racket coming from outside. It sounded like a truck backfiring. As my father and I stepped out the front door, an old beat up truck pulled in the driveway. It was an older man that lived just down the road, Willy Summers. A few years back there was a flood. The water swept through the creek banks and washed a whole section off of his fence line off. Not only did my father help round up all of Willy's cattle, but he also helped the following week reinstalling the fence. There was only one reason Willy usually came around. He must have needed help, because something bad must had happened.

"Willy," my father acknowledged him as he stepped out of his truck. "What can I do for you?"

"Well, Samuel," Willy said as he shook my father's hand. "I brought you a thank you gift. You know for helping me during the flood," he continued as we walked to the back of his truck. "At about 5:30 this morning I was startled awake by a loud noise that sounded like a car wreck. Somehow Mable crossed the cattle guard in my front yard and that old drunk Sal Bonder hit her with his truck."

"Oh, crap," I interrupted. "Who's Mable?"

"My cow," Willy answered. "Well, she was my cow. Now she's a couple of boxes of steaks for your dinner table. I would have been here sooner, but I stopped down at Sal's place. I mean, he just hit my cow and drove off. After a while he got around to asking me what I was going to do with the meat. As soon as I told him I was going to bring it to you, he ran into his kitchen. He grabbed a box and told me to give it to you as well. Now I won't lie to you, I took a peek in there, and he gave you a full box of . . ."

"Potatoes," I interjected.

"Well yes," Willy stared at me in disbelief.

"And this all happened this morning?" My father asked.

"Yeah, it all began around 5 . . ."

"Was it 5:21?" I asked.

"You know what?" Willy stopped for a moment to refresh his memory. "When I jumped out of bed from the sound of the wreck, I came face to face with my clock. And believe it or not it was exactly 5:21. How did you know that?" Willy asked as he stared at me with that same strange look of disbelief.

"I don't know," I answered.

Many could question that what had happened was nothing more than circumstantial. But in my eyes, the facts were indisputable. Even if I wanted to say it was incidental, I gave my word to God. He kept his end of the bargain by providing my family with food and I would keep my end of the agreement.

After opening my eyes, in my bedroom, back in reality. I began to follow the steps I had been taking. I followed the direction my life took, from that morning of miracles, to my life now as a delinquent. Did everything have to work out like it did? Could I have taken the wrong path? Where would I be if something else would have happened?

As much as I would like to believe that my life would have been different if I had changed an aspect of my life. The truth is that there was one turning point in my life. No matter how I add my life up in different directions. There is only one common denominator in my life. The days that I spent my 78 hour hiatus from civilization at the cemetery was the alter point. The discovery behind Eddie's death would always be the major factor in my life.

I walked in the house after seeing the smudge on the back of Eddie's car and knelt down at that same alter that I had used to give my heart to God. I prayed for guidance and deliverance from my own evil thoughts. When I didn't receive anything in return, I decided to take matters into my own hands. My prayers went from beautiful and wondrous remarks of my Lord and savior; to hateful vindictive comments like, "Fine don't help. But you better stay out of my way or I swear. You will not like the direction my life turns to next!" I continued to be that way until I slowly stopped praying all together. It was much easier to think in a different manner. Not that I reformed back to not believing in him at all. My mind would never change after that Monday morning of miracles. But I now believed that God didn't care about me or my problems. It was so much easier to believe that he/she was more or less toying with me. Only because I felt that he/she was not allowing me to receive the satisfaction I so desperately desired.

It took me a while to regroup after my acknowledgment of things that would never change. At times like these when I am reminiscing in my mind, it usually takes a few minutes for me to get back up to speed on life still occurring around me. On occasion, I have to stop for a moment just so I can remember to breathe. During this juncture I just needed to remember why I was going through all of it in the first place. I was trying to change my life's direction. But with my mind riddled with painful conclusions of how my life turned out. I apparently needed to take a break.

Chapter 13

After a slight break of lunch, I eventually made my way back to my room to think of the last story. I didn't contemplate for long, on what my final story would be. It was a simple deduction to what is now my favorite story up to this point in my life. The story is how Eddie turned from nemesis, to ally. The collaboration had only one turning point, high school. On the first day of my freshman year, Eddie gave me five guidelines to help me survive the adjustment.

"There are some rules we need to go over before you enter this establishment. First rule," Eddie stopped me before we headed into the school. "No one needs to know that we are brothers. Number two; if you mess with one chocolate chip, you have to deal with the whole cookie," he said. At the time I didn't understand the rule completely, but I definitely would later that day. "Stay low and for God sakes stay out of trouble. The third rule; do not under any circumstances, try to be a hero and help someone that is being picked on. Rule number four; if anyone approaches you and is talking about drugs. Don't even utter a word to them, just grab your things, and walk away. The fifth and final rule is something I'm not truly worried about with you, but I will state it regardless. Do not talk about God. This is not summer camp and this is not our church group. We may believe in God, but that does not mean that everyone else does. If you abide by these rules you should be fine, but the first rule is the only one I care about. You must never break rule number one, for if you do, I will break you."

I was doing fine until I got to my third class of the day. I was sitting next to the door of the classroom, with my hands holding my head up. Needless to say I was bored. I hated everything about school. Even on big exam days, I felt a little lackluster. I would flip through exams in a couple of minutes and spend the rest of the time staring out the window. I would always make sure that I got a few of the answers wrong so that no one would ask any questions. If you didn't know, when taking an exam and you get every question right; rumors start up that you must have cheated. Then when they find out the truth, they want you to take tests to skip grades. The same thing happened to both Eddie and I in elementary. Like we would want to skip grades and head off for college before we were even able to drive.

As I debated on whether or not to fall asleep, I eavesdropped in on a conversation between the teacher and a fellow student. The student, R.J., was a football player. He was older than I was, by a couple of years. Not to make it sound like he was stupid or something because he was in a freshman class. But he was more or less burning time until he turned eighteen so he could drop out of school and get his G.E.D. He had already spent too much time messing around in school. It was his best chance of getting into community college without having to wait until he was twenty-one to graduate from high school. At least this is what he planned on doing after this semester, basically after the football season.

The discussion didn't seem important at the time but it would definitely be needful information for later. The teacher didn't really seem interested in the conversation but more or less needed to find something to help pass the time. So she asked, "Are we going to make the playoffs this year?"

I desperately wanted to join their little chat but I did not. I don't know what it is that draws me to football, but I love the sport. It might have had something to do with my mother not wanting me to play the blood sport. Apparently that only made it more desirable in my mind. She always said it was too dangerous for me. For if she only knew what I did now for a living. Slinging ice to skeezer's (my word for someone who gives their life away to drugs.), who would much rather cut your face off and steal your supply, than pay the five bucks for the bump. It's crazy how things change in only a few years.

Anyway, as their conversation carried on, I began to turn my attention to what was happening outside the window. Not that I was easily distracted, but because of the way I was raised. It was considered rude to jump into the middle of a conversation. In my family there was a huge difference between conversation and discussion. Conversation was a chat between two or maybe three people. And if you were not introduced as an insightful third or fourth party, you didn't join in on your own recognition. Or basically, you couldn't input until you were acknowledged. Now discussion, on the other hand, is a collaboration of various other persons and an assortment of other opinions. Much like a class room discussion, where the topic could continually change, and opinions may vary.

As I blankly stared out the window, an intruder tried to breach their exchange of words. "Yeah, but our defense kind of sucks," she interrupted. She cut down R.J. and our coaching staff. Yet with her demeanor of saying continually, "I mean, it's not you R.J. There are ten other people out there that just really suck." For some odd reason she still seemed to seek his approval. As if she would give some insightful input in exchange for some sort of popularity. Apparently, she didn't understand how becoming popular worked. There are five types of popularity: the first is being easy in the bedroom department and it really does not matter what gender you are for it either. The second is being a school work horse. You know, striding in excellence for school pride. Keep in mind that sometimes this type of approval seeking does not work. The third is by just being a good person. This type of approval has only one setback to it and that's if you are too nice. If you don't have a backbone in high school, you will be run over every time someone receives the opportunity. The fourth is someone who does not really seek approval, yet they receive it from the opposite sex for being attractive. The final person inquiring support from fellow companions is the Jerk or the Witch, gaining approval by mean spirited cut downs.

This girl didn't seem to contain any of these qualities. Now R.J. on the other hand was a popular person. Along with being a part of the fifth characteristic, over the years he had also obtained the first as well.

"What would you know?" R.J. answered defending himself and his team. "You just sit your fat gelatin rump roast in the stands and watch from a distance! You're not on the field to see what we have to do, you don't know a thing!"

As the teacher stood up, I thought she was going to put an end to the conversation. But apparently she thought it would be a good time to use the restroom. As R.J. continued to give the girl a hard time, I decided that I might need to interrupt. I didn't want to, but somebody needed to say something. "So you believe she doesn't know anything regarding the football team?" I stopped his outburst.

"Yes and you can shut up too!" He yelled.

"Come on now, I'm actually being nice," I laughed at him. "Now answer me this. Who knows more about football, you or the coach?"

"Well of course Coach does," he answered.

"Well here's a fact for you that you may not have known," I continued. "The head football coach at this school has never played a down in his life. He learned the game of football by watching and learning in college. Now with keeping that in mind, all she was doing was making an observation from her seat in the stands. She may even know more about football than you do."

"That's ridiculous!" He laughed off the statement.

"Ok," I began again. "Ridiculous or not, from watching our football team from last year, she is right about the defense. It did suck. Your D line is to fat and it doesn't have enough speed to apply any pressure. Your blitz package is screwed because you can only blitz linebackers. Leaving the DB's to pick up zone coverage because the safeties are too slow for man coverage. And it's even worse when you blitz the corners because your free safety is so slow mentally and physically, a wide receiver blows past him every time. I believe his name is Blackwolf . . ." I stopped myself. I had already gone too far and was unable to stop in time. I had instantaneously remembered something from when R.J. entered the room. He walked in wearing his Letterman jacket and as I looked around to see how many class mates I had. I saw his last name on the back of his jacket, which by ill-fated coincidence was Blackwolf.

As I looked at his enraged facial expression, I instantly felt the need to run, and I did. Right out the door, down the hallway and towards the library. As I opened the door to the library, I turned around to see R.J. closing in on me. I rushed towards the self help section and

79

grabbed a book on self defense. Hints how I learned how to fight. I flipped through it quickly, visualizing myself doing every move, when I looked up to see an onlooker. He looked surprised, yet doubtful that I had read the entire book in just a matter of seconds. Yet again, I covered five hundred pages, and that's not really that big of an obstacle. You should see me breeze through encyclopedias. I slowly made my way back to the main doors, when the librarian stopped me. "Can I help you?" She asked.

"Ah," I stuttered as I saw R.J. enter the library. "Yes you can. I'm looking for some information on steroid abuse. How it causes hair loss? Why it causes users to become inept to sexual partners? And how it leads to homosexual tendencies?"

"Oh, ok," she answered with a strange look on her face. "Right over here." As I followed her, I looked back to see R.J. give me the universal sign for death as he slid his thumb across his throat. It was basically to let me know that I would most likely die later today. And just to anger him and make things a little more interesting. I, in return, blew him a kiss and winked at him.

After scanning a few books, I heard the bell ring for lunch. As I made my way out into the hallway, I didn't notice R.J. anywhere. I instantly let out a sigh of relief as I made my way to the cafeteria. "I don't really need to be getting into a fight on my first day of school," I told myself. "But on the positive side. It could be exciting. Who else could say they got into a fight on their first day of high school?" I began to get thrilled with the opportunity. Not only would it be my first fight in school, but it would also be my first fight altogether. I was so exuberant about the thought of it all, that I felt like I could no longer wait to see R.J. again. Fortunately, my wait was short lived, for I received exactly what I wanted as I entered the lunchroom.

R.J. stared me down for a few moments and then told me, "Indianola, 4 o'clock, today." I didn't really want to wait that long to make him look like a prepubescent momma's boy, but I kind of needed to. My father would be very upset if I got into a fight in school. And R.J. didn't really need the trouble of fighting either. So we both needed to wait.

I spent the remainder of the day preparing for my battle. I used my eidetic memory to go over and over the pages of the self defense book.

Even at the end of the school day, while I was headed to Eddie's car, I continued to go over the different techniques. I barely got slipped into the passenger side seat of the car, before Eddie began to take off. For some odd reason he was hurrying along to get me back to the house.

"Ah, Eddie," I said. "Is there any reason why you're rushing around?"

"Yeah, I need to hurry and get you home. I have some where I need to be," he answered.

"And that would be?"

"Ah," he stuttered on whether or not to tell me. "There's supposed to be a fight after school. A buddy of mine, R.J. Blackwolf, is going to pound some freshman. I don't know who would be stupid enough to irritate him that badly, but I seriously feel sorry for them. He's kind of a mad man."

"Oh, come on Eddie! I want to go watch the fight," I pleaded. I didn't want to tell him that I was the one that was going to fight, because he never would have allowed me to go. "It's just a fight. I promise to stay out of the way."

"If I take you," he interjected. "You must promise that mom and dad will never find out about it."

"I promise," I answered with a smile.

The fight was taking place at Indianola school house. It was an abandoned school building, from the early 1800's, just outside of town. Places like this were secluded and made it easy to isolate the noise. It also made it easy to keep the various persons away that might want to put a halt to the massacre; much like the police, school faculty that found out about it, and parents of the assailants. There were a couple of other places around town that had the same seclusion. Of course there was old abandoned schools, another place was Beer Can Mountain, and last but not least Condom Pond.

After arriving at Indianola, Eddie gave me specific instructions to walk around the crowd, and stand in a truck bed so that I could watch. As he walked away, I slowly made my way through the mob, continually slipping in between, and nudging people out of my way. The closer I became to the center of the crowd, the more electrifying their demeanor became. As a dispute broke out, of whether or not I had showed, I pushed my way through the remaining outer shell and into the inner circle. "Don't worry, I'm here," I said.

"Good, I thought you might have chickened out," R.J. answered back.

"Look, I must have hurt your pride or something. I didn't mean to. I'm sorry for what happened today and I take back every word of it . . ."

"Are you trying to back out?" R.J. laughed.

"Heavens no, I'm just apologizing. I just wanted to give you the chance to walk away," I interrupted his chuckle as I began to step closer. "We can still do this."

"Ooh, big talker, can you back it up?"

"Enough talk. Let's do this?" I said.

Instead of smarting off and making fun of him, I should have been paying attention to my surroundings. For if I had, I would have heard the two Neanderthals walk up behind me. They grabbed my arms, and lead me to R.J., restraining me from retaliation. It was a cowardly move, but I should have expected it. R.J. was a dirty football player and apparently a dirty fighter as well.

After being dragged to R.J. he then struck me once in the stomach with an uppercut. I had never been hit before, but his rock hard fist made me want to reveal my lunch. The excruciating pain shot through my tense upper body. Thus releasing a heap of adrenaline into my system and freeing my will to contain my emotions. I cried out as his fist collided with my face, and a single tear rolled down my face as he struck me again on the cheek. As I faltered wondering what I should do for my reprisal, I had an instant feeling of fear creep into my mind. I wasn't terrified of the beating I had been receiving but instead of the monster they had awakened inside of me. I looked into the eyes of my attacker and noticed he looked like he had been caught in astonishment for a moment. As I looked to my right, I found out why he had such a strange reaction. Eddie had knocked out the assailant that had been holding one of my arms. With my now free arm I did the same to the guy on the left of me, before I fell to my knee.

"What the . . . Eddie?" R.J. barked. "What are you doing?"

"Helping my brother," Eddie answered as he continued to let everyone know. "That's right, this is my little brother. And if you want to mess with him you have to go through me . . ."

"It's ok," I cut Eddie off. "I can do this."

"Are you sure?" Eddie asked.

"Of course, and don't worry I'll make it quick. I know we have chores to do back at the house," I answered. As I stood up, I spit out a mouthful of blood, and took my fighting stance.

One would think that doing a back flip is easier than it looks, but it is quite the opposite. When I jumped planting my right foot into R.J.'s face, I forgot to plan in the force it would take to make it back around. The problem wasn't that I didn't use enough force, but instead I used too much. I landed on my heels almost falling to my back.

"Oh, you want to kick," he exclaim. "Let me show you something then."

Apparently, he wanted to show me how not to kick someone. A right foot to the ribs is usually intended to weaken the opponent or maybe at most break a rib. I caught his telegraphed kick, with my left arm, and punched him in the scrotum with the right. After regaining some bearings he again came at me. As he did, I nonchalantly slapped him in the throat and watched him fall to his knees gasping for air. I didn't want to hurt him, but I was no longer in control of my emotions. The fight was basically over, but I continued regardless. I followed up the throat slap with an uppercut. He flew backwards landing on, what seemed like, the back of his head. The final blow had finally rendered him unconscious. I never saw R.J. again after the fight. The uppercut had broken his jaw, thus making his approach to community college and life after high school; begin a little sooner than he had planned.

"William!" My father yelled waking me up from my day dream.

"On my way Pops," I answered him.

"Before you start, I want to give you one last chance to tell me what happened last night," he said as I sat down in the chair next to him.

I couldn't tell him the truth I promised Lynn that I wouldn't tell anyone. And I most defiantly didn't want to lie to him anymore either. So I decided to change the subject. It would most likely enrage my father, but in return maybe I could come up with something that would make him think. "Wait," I stopped. "You expect me to stand here and elaborate on things I've learned, in hopes to change me or make me a better person. I mean for God sakes you gave me an ultimatum to either change or get out. My question to you is, when exactly do you begin to change? We both know you've always treated this family like it was just something to pass the time, as if you are waiting for greener pastures . . ."

"I don't know what your mother has told you . . ." he began.

"Do you really think I give a crap about what my mother thinks about you?" I stopped him. "If I have a problem with you, it is because of something you've done. Please, don't think I'm simple minded enough to be persuaded for or against someone by the views of someone other than my own." As our battle of wits continued I began doing something I believed I would never do. I began to rummage through my father's mind looking for a weakness to end the conversation. I didn't want to but it needed to be done. After scanning a few conversations in different directions, I finally landed on what made my father tick. His pride in Eddie and I was my foot in the door. "You blame me," I continued. "You blame me for making you leave Oklahoma!"

"I don't blame you," he said as his mind scrambled for an answer that wouldn't cast guilt in my direction. "Maybe I'm just a free spirit and felt like leaving?"

"Yeah, maybe you're right," I answered. "Maybe you are a free spirit. Do you want to know what word I associate with free spirit," I continued as he acknowledged, "Quitter."

"Alright, enough, let's calm down now."

"Yeah, we don't want to let the truth come out."

"I don't like your tone, boy."

"You don't like my tone. You don't like my abilities. Tell the truth dad, you don't like anything about me, do you?"

"I didn't say that!"

"You don't have to. I can read you like an open book," I answered. "If you don't like the way I act or who I am. Then maybe you shouldn't have raised me to be this way!" Blaming my parents for my shortcomings is something I, again, thought I would never do. It is one thing to know that your parents are to blame for your faults, because denying the fact would be foolish. But to actually tell a parent that they are at fault is an unemotionally shallow façade. Only meant to hinder and deeply wound the intended parental. "Check mate, Pops," I told myself as he lowered his head in shame.

"I'm sorry, Will," my father said.

"Don't be," I answered trying to lift his spirits. I was already beginning to wish that I hadn't said what I had just told him. "In the end you have only made me stronger and able to stand on my own two feet. In my quest for answers today, I searched for stories of what you wanted me to think about, family. But in my search, I discovered my own strengths. Thanks to Mrs. Sullivan, I have the intellectual will power to think before I act. My prayer for food at age nine gave me a well needed strength in spirit. And my first altercation in school showed me I had the strength to stand toe to toe with just about anyone physically. But honestly, you are right. I do have one weakness. I don't really have any family. Not that I'm "declaring emancipation" from you and mom either. But I am saying I cannot do this alone. I will need help. Just . . . don't give up on me Pops. I know I may not be getting everything right, but I'm not getting everything wrong either.

Chapter 14

As I stepped out of the truck, I continually took deep breathes. I knew what I had to do as I walked towards the class room. I had to apologize to Elizabeth for the incident at the school. Although I would never admit it, she believed I was wrong. So I needed to make things right. Then, I had to find a way to tell her that I wasn't going to be able to spend the day with her. Even though she was still mad at me, I remained optimistic to the idea that she still wanted me to go to the beach with her. So in theory, I had to lie to her because I didn't believe that I was wrong. Also, on a completely different occasion I had caused my father enough anguish to lead him to ground me.

I had just made it around the corner of the building, when I saw her standing in the doorway. "Hey . . ." I said as she turned towards me. "I just wanted to say . . ."

"I'm sorry," she blurted out. "I shouldn't have been mad at you for, doing what you thought was right."

"No," I replied, "I should have just grabbed you and walked away, instead of starting a fight."

"I was a little scared . . ."

"I was a little pushy . . ."

"So we're good?" I asked as she acknowledged.

Elizabeth stunned me by how easy it was for her to forgive. Little did I know it wouldn't be the last time she would surprise me today. "Lynn and I talked last night after she got home . . ." She started. Apparently, Lynn had finally told someone about what had happened, "Good for her," I thought. Someone else needed to know other than myself. I never was much of a touchy feely person. The only problem was that now I would need to explain myself to Elizabeth. Why I was at the party? What was my affiliation to the idiots that had done those things to Lynn? And above all else, why didn't I stop it earlier? "She just said," She continued to explain, "That I can't be mad at you for being barbaric. I guess the more I thought about it, the clearer it became. In some situations, it's a good quality."

"Well . . . Thank you . . . I think," I replied with a confused look. She didn't ask any of the questions that I had assumed she would ask. Maybe her characteristics were beginning to change. I had to admit that even my own outlook on life was beginning to change. As if I was becoming comfortable in my own skin around her and her family. The adaptation was new. I had never really felt, well, happy. So there was really no comparison to decide whether I loved or hated my new environment. "Hey, I'll meet you inside," I said as I saw David walk around the corner.

I was a little angry that David wanted to get away from Matt. But who was I to be mad at him? If I didn't have an ulterior motive, I wouldn't be doing it either. "I know this is probably the last thing you want to hear, but I believe it's time to stop," he explained.

"I understand," I replied, "and I'm sorry for making things crazy these last couple of weeks."

"Don't be, it'll probably be the best thing that's ever happened to me," he laughed. "So what really happened at the party?" He asked.

I had sworn to Lynn, that I would never speak about that night ever again, not even to her. She was worried that if David found out he would end up going to prison, for tracking down and killing everyone that was at the party. I just let it go and said, "You'll have to ask Lynn. I can't really say anymore than that or I'll break a promise to a close friend."

I had bigger problems to worry about anyway. I had to find a way to tell Elizabeth that I would not be going with her today. My mind ran ramped for at least 17 hours nonstop, thinking of how I could get out of my grounding. And many times, before last night's release from reflective sentencing. I would come to the same conclusion that I had when my parents split up. My father is a top notch pompous antagonizing sphincter that does not care about anyone but himself.

I know it is strange for me to think of things that way, but analyzing him as a jerk, was much easier than admitting that I might have been wrong. For if I was wrong. That would make my father right. And that conundrum in itself would undo the world as we know it. Before last night, this would have ultimately been my conclusion. But my outlook on my father and my surroundings were beginning to change.

"And how do you feel about it William?" Mrs. Maples asked.

"I'm sorry . . ." I answered. I had sat down for the class to begin, and did not even think twice about it actually starting. The class had begun nearly twenty minutes ago and I did not have the foggiest idea of what they had been talking about. "What were we talking about?" I asked.

"Sex," she said, as the entire class turned its attention towards me. Everyone there had seen what I had done two weeks ago. But for some odd reason, I could not stay focused. I had tunnel vision or something of that nature. My mind would not allow me to do more than one thing at a time.

"Well," I answered. "Sex is just another addiction that mankind cannot seem to get under control. For a female it gets pretty bad when all of your friends have had sex. Before you know it, you begin to get a little curious and your friends start telling you 'it's just sex. Quit thinking so much about it, and just do it.' So you finally do. Then the rumors start circling of you being easy and how you give it up to everyone," I continued. "But for the male gender it's even worse. Once you do have sex. If you don't lay with every presumably STD infested girl that seems interested, then you're gay. It would be ok if it was someone you didn't like, pressuring you into these types of situations, because then you could easily walk away. But it's not. It's coming from your so-called friends."

"Ok, thank you Will," Mrs. Maples cut me off.

"I'm not done yet," I replied. "It's the generation we're growing up in. A hundred years ago, you never even talked about sex. And honestly they didn't even have sex, unless the couple was married. And even then, they would only have sex if they were planning on having children.

Now along with the problem of young people having sex and the possibilities of spreading new diseases, we have branched off to various other problems. Like child pornography from young people emailing and texting nude photos of themselves to their boy/girl friends. And I get it, sex sells, and these young people are trying to sell themselves. Most of them are selling their physical appearance to their boyfriends or girlfriends. They are showing what they believe to be their sexiness. In the long run, all they are hoping is that they will not be looked over by their partner. When their partner believes they have seen greener pastures, they will send them their sexual pictures. And how should these children know that these kinds of actions are wrong. When there is something of a sexual nature, in every direction you turn. It's in music, movies, and even regular programmed television. When we figure it out, we began to cast blame everywhere we can. Is it the musicians' fault that he wanted to show people the truths in life that he has learned by putting them into rhymes? But the only way he could show the world his genius works was by writing a song about pimps, hoes, and taking drugs in the club. Is it the director's fault that he wanted to bare his soul in a film? But the only way it would sell, is if he put in a sex scene. Is it the broadcasting companies fault that the only way they could compete with the more major channels, was to show a little skin. You can point the finger and cast blame as much as you want to, but you by God better be looking in a mirror! It is our fault. As a whole, it is entirely our fault!"

It did not take long for me to figure out that something was wrong. It had seemed that when I focused on something, it was the only thing I could think about. I started thinking about talking to Elizabeth and I could not hear anything going on in class. I focused my attention out the window and I could not think. Although I had done nothing wrong, my S.S.T.S.T. photographic memory and multi-tasking ability's were gone.

"What's wrong William?" Mrs. Maples asked.

Yet again I was not paying attention and the classroom had been empty for a few minutes now. "I don't know," I answered.

"You seem a little out of your element," Elizabeth said with a sympathetic look.

"Ah!!!" I screamed as the visions and thoughts came screaming back into my mind. As before, my eyes began to blur, as I fell to the floor of the class room. And I again began having the same dream I had last time I was here.

I was there in the strange bed, just like before. As the scream echoed in the room, I stood up and headed for the door. When all of the sudden the scream echoed again. In the hallway now, I see the green piece of construction paper with Eddie's name on it. Deeply confused, I took a deep breath before I entered. Just like before, the blinding light rushed through the door, but it quickly began to fade. I saw Elizabeth sitting in a rocking chair, she looked very tired. She was holding something in her arms but I could not make out what it was. As I stepped around to view the object, I saw her holding an infant. As she looked up, she smiled and said, "Would you like to hold your son?" My heart began to pound loudly as I opened my eyes there in the classroom. Just as I had seen it in my dreams, that same loving smile met me as I awoke. For Elizabeth was standing over me looking down.

"Are you ok?" Elizabeth asked.

"I think so," I replied. I had actually never felt better. I quickly stood up, walked to the couch, and sat down. "What's on the agenda for today, Mrs. Maples?"

"Nothing," she answered. "I have some things to do, so we are going to be taking the day off. That and I believe you two were planning on spending the day at the beach, right."

"Yes, about that," I answered as I turned my attention towards Elizabeth. "I can't go. My father heard from the school . . ." I did not even get to finish what I was saying. It looked like I had awakened a sleeping monster because Mrs. Maples was already headed out the door. *"She looks like a woman on a mission,"* I thought as I followed her up the sidewalk. As she reached my father, she began explaining to him about what had happened at the school and our plans for a peaceful day at the beach. Apparently, Elizabeth had told her all about the altercation at school and after speaking to him for a few minutes, she waved me over.

"Is that true Will?" My father asked. "Were you just sticking up for someone?"

"Yes sir," I answered. "I tried to tell you but . . ."

"Its ok." he stopped me. "Would you excuse us for a moment ladies?"

"Yes, no problem," Mrs. Maples answered.

"I guess you won't be standing on the sidelines anymore," my father said as I shot him a strange look. "You know you don't have to be a psychic to know somebody," my father continued. "You said something that caught my attention last night. You said, 'I might not be getting everything right, but I'm not getting everything wrong either.' But it certainly feels that way. You've been watching this game of life pass you by for years and it got even worse after your brother passed. You sit and wait, and then you sit and wait some more. I know you don't get everything wrong, but almost every time you have an opportunity to do something, it is wrong. And it almost feels like you are lashing out at your mother and me, for something we did wrong."

"I'm sorry Pops, I don't mean to make it seem that way."

"I know you don't, but at least you're headed in the right direction now."

"What makes you think I'm headed in the right direction this time?"

"Well," he answered. "It's not every day that I get threatened by a sixty year old woman, for something my son did right. Look, we'll talk more about this later, when you get home from the beach." I have seen my father make many facial expressions before. From anger and sadness, to happiness and forgetful, but this was a new one. Not to say that I never saw it before. I had seen it bestowed upon Eddie's many remarkable accomplishments in the past. With a slight grin and his eyes welling up a little, I knew what the look was for, pride. My father for the first time in my lifetime was actually sincerely proud of me. In his eyes I had finally done something right. I gave up trying to get my father's approval a long time ago. It was nearly impossible to get any recognition for anything when you have someone like Eddie as an older brother. *"I'm proud of me too,"* I thought to myself as I read my father's thoughts.

Chapter 15

As I sat in my truck, I continued to hope and pray that my fears would not come true. I had been to the beach once before and it did not seem to work out entirely all that well. And unless Elizabeth had a bottle of whiskey in her purse, I was screwed. I could not help but to think that this could have been a mistake.

"Hey," I said trying to get her attention before she stepped out of the vehicle. "I have a problem with the beach . . ."

"What's the problem?" She asked. "Maybe I can help."

"Last time I was here, my mind was racing, and everything kind of hit me all at once. It was a lot of mind numbing pain," I explained.

"Ok, why don't you take it one step at a time?" she answered. "Focus on one thing until you get used to it and then focus on something else. Here this might help with the sound," She said as she handed me her I-pod.

"One thing at a time," I continually reminded myself as I began to step out of the truck. I could not help but to think that I looked like a five year old going off the deep end of the pool, as I pushed myself out of the truck. I was holding my nose tight with my hand, I had a type of ear plugs on, and my eyes were shut. *"Ok, smell goes first,"* I told myself. It was the only logical choice. Only because it would make it harder to complete the other four tasks. How would I ever expect to finish, if I was unconscious on the ground, just because I decided to stop breathing?

Next was sight. But only because I was tired of looking like a complete idiot. *"Wow, it looks like a beach,"* I laughed. To be completely honest it was very beautiful. The day was turning into a day that neither of us were very likely to forget anytime soon.

After sight was taste. For the soul reason of it being the simplest task. I reached down picked up a grain of sand and stuck it in my mouth. Of course it tasted like sand, but there subtle hints of other flavorings. There was a dash of salt, a hint of dirty feet, and a smidgen of what I believed to be fish guts. I do not know exactly what the guts of a fish or the bottom of someone's feet taste like. But I am pretty sure it tasted like whatever was in my mouth.

I quickly took my shoes off, to get started on touch, and walked down by the shore. I did not take long to find out that the temperature of the sand changed in certain areas. Down by the water it was nice and cool, and back where I had parked was about thirty degrees warmer. It was different and took some getting used to, but I managed.

Last but not least, sound. The first four senses were relatively easy to make it through. I knew that sound was going to be the toughest that is why I made it the last task. As I pulled off the head phones from Elizabeth's I-pod, the first wave crashed against the shoreline. I tried to focus, but it was a little too much for me to take in. I quickly stuck the head phones back on, and closed my eyes tight. I instantly fell to my knees as I continued to try and stop the images from scrambling my brain like an egg.

"Focus on me, big deep breathes," Elizabeth yelled over the music. I do not know exactly what I was listening to but I immediately turned it up trying to block out all of the noise. Frustrated and prepared to give up on the endeavor. I instantly began trying to control my breathing as I heard Elizabeth yelling over the music. "Think of the beach as a beautiful song you love to hear. And the waves crashing are more like the drum beat."

It took awhile for me to start, but I began thinking about my favorite song, and gradually pulled off the head phones. It had worked just like she had said it would. My mind had completely slowed down. I felt a slight breeze coming from off of the ocean. I could smell the salty residue in the air and I could hear the seagull's flying from up above me. And along with the other senses working clearly, the sound was the most incredible. It sounded like a beautiful medley that Mother Nature had prepared that was meant for my ears only. Everybody was right, the beach was relaxing. "Thank you," I said to Elizabeth.

"You're welcome," she answered with a grin.

At first I could not pin point exactly what I loved most about the beach. Was it the beautiful shells washing up to shore? The calming feeling I had when the waves crashed against the shore? Or was it the foot massage I was receiving from the sand and waves rushing in between my toes? For my first time being at the beach without being inebriated, I had to admit, I had never been more at peace. Shortly thereafter, I found out exactly what I loved the most about the beach and she was staring right back at me.

As we walked down the beach, I had Elizabeth ask me random questions. Just to see if my memory, withstood the so called "calmness" of the beach. Not that I would actually need it today, but you could never be sure what might come around the corner. "What's your favorite color?" Elizabeth asked.

"Blue," I answered. "What's yours?"

"Although I wear a lot of pink and red, my favorite color is purple. But you already knew that," she replied. "Have you ever heard the expression, 'The greatest story's ever told are through the eyes of a tortured soul.'"

"Of course, why do you ask?"

"Tell me a story."

"Ouch! You don't hold anything back do you? I like it."

"Sorry, I don't mean to push your buttons or anything. It just seems that is who you truly are, a tortured soul." She was not completely wrong in her assessment. I have been beating myself up for years. About things that were not my fault and of things I could not control.

"Ok," I paused while I thought about what story to tell her. "After hanging out with Anthony and Justin, for about a week . . ."

"No! I do not want to hear anything bad. I want to hear a good story," she replied.

"Do you have any suggestions?" I questioned.

"I want to hear the most romantic story you've ever heard," She answered.

I instantly knew what story I was going to tell her. But I took a moment, hoping I would think of something else. The story had sentimental value and was only supposed to be told on certain occasions. Nothing else came to mind so I began, "Ok," I smiled. "I will tell you the story, but keep in mind you must never tell my father I told you."

"No problem, your secret is safe with me," she mocked me.

"Ok," I said. "Til' the end of day's."

"Why? Til' the end of day's?"

"My mother had it inscribed on her wedding ring, by my father. And my grandmother had it etched on a plank of wood, by my grandfather. It still hangs there just above the front door of their house. My grandmother told me she left it above the door so that all people traveling by would know that it was a house of love and compassion." I regretted giving her the opportunity to pick the story. I should have told her a hunting story about Eddie, our grandfather, and myself. But it was too late to change my mind now.

"Ok," she said, "and the story behind it?"

Chapter 16

When I was about ten years old, we went on vacation. To see my grandparent's in Colorado. When we first arrived, I saw the piece of wood on my way through the door, and I actually thought the world was coming to an end. I grabbed Eddie's arm and asked him what it meant, but he just told me to ask Grandpa. One night when it was just my grandfather and I, I asked him about it.

He told me, that when his father (My great grandfather and his name was William, also) was about eight years old. He met a young girl named Katherine, (my great grandmother) who was seven. By chance, Katherine's family moved into a house about a half a mile away. Although that may seem like a long distance to live apart from someone now days, that made Katherine, William's closest neighbor.

One day, while on their way home after fishing in the nearby creek, Katherine asked William if he knew what love was. William had asked himself the same question many times before. Contemplating the dimensions on what he believed love to be. He did the only thing that came to mind. He asked his mother what it was and he replied with the same answer his mother had given him. "Love is when you cannot live without someone."

Katherine let it register in her mind for a moment before she complied, "In that case, I love you."

Days turned into months, and months into years. And before long, they were teenagers. And other than sleep and work, William spent every waking moment with her. Neither one of them had even felt the need to make more friends. It seemed like they had decided to take on the world by themselves. On one summer Saturday while fishing at that same nearby creek. Katherine told William again, like many times before, that she loved him.

William thought for a moment and before replied, "and I you, til' the end of days." It was the first time William had announced his love for her. The words had seemed so sacred to him. That it had taken him this long, to even utter different words with the same meaning. She instantly blushed and acknowledged how hard it must have been for him.

That same day, Williams' father, (basically the town drunk) came home with a horse that he had apparently, "just found." William immediately recognized the horse's brand. For he had seen it many times before that day, it was Katherine's fathers. Bent on changing his ways, so he did not end up like his father, William took the horse back. When he explained what had happened, to Katherine's father, he did not believe William. As William walked away ashamed of his father, Katherine ran out of the house, and began yelling to William that she loved him.

He replied, "and I you, til' the end of days."

None of it had mattered anyway. William and Katherine were married, only a year later. During the ceremony, when the pastor asked William to repeat after him, William waved him off. He said, "Love is too sacred for me to repeat the same thing everyone else always says. I will love you and you alone, forever. More than anyone will ever love anyone else and until death do us part is not long enough for me. I say, til' the end of days. I believe that should be long enough for our love."

My grandfather then told me that he was only twelve years old when his mother passed away. Katherine's death would eventually tear the family apart. William had problems trying to deal with life after his wife's death. But William found a new purpose in life, when Katherine's father tried to pay for the funeral. Much like he tried to pay for everything else over the years, William denied the favor. William told him that he himself would take care of it. William knowing he needed to handle this on his own. Set off immediately to speak with the town undertaker.

William made a deal with the undertaker. I exchange for the tombstone and lessons on how to chisel words into the stone. William would dig every hole, for every funeral, for free, for one year. William worked two jobs that year. During the day, he worked at the saw mill just outside of town. And every night, as he had promised, he dug every hole in the cemetery. At nearly day break, after the last night of a full year worth of digging graves, William made his way to Katherine's burial site. It was all the way back down by the same creek they had spent their childhood at. Under a tree right next to their favorite fishing hole was where she was laid to rest. And with his hammer and Chisel, he carved the words, "Til' the end of days" into her tombstone.

Our family, after that year, prided ourselves on how much he loved her. He pushed himself to the limits for her and if he were still alive he would still tell you it was worth it. But from then on, the words became sacred, and a piece of our history.

My grandfather then told me that he said those same words to my grandmother one night, and then told her the story behind it. He then followed up the evening by asking for my grandmother's hand in marriage. And like my family before me, I shall use those same words, on the night I ask the woman of my dreams the ultimate question.

"That was by far the most beautiful thing I've ever heard," Elizabeth said as she wiped a tear from her eyes. "Thank you, Will."

"What's with the tears?" I asked. "It seems like every time we talk, you're shedding tears. Maybe it would be a good idea if we did not speak together," I laughed. "You ask a question, and I will just nod or something."

"I'm an emotional person. When I hear or see something beautiful, or sad, I can't control myself nor would I want to try. It's kind of like an adventurous person and how they do something crazy. Like base jumping off of a building, going swimming with the sharks, or sky diving. I let my emotions take the best of me, because I want to feel the pain and anguish or the love and happiness. I do it so that I can make sure that I am still alive and not just boring myself with the same old bull crap."

Chapter 17

"How 'bout a swim?" Elizabeth asked as she began shedding her clothes down to her bathing suit. As I began to take my shirt off. I stopped and began thinking about what had happened to get me to this point. From the trouble I had gotten into in Oklahoma, to me sitting on the beach with the most beautiful girl I had ever seen. She was so pure, so innocent, but yet she was edgy enough to call me on my own stupidity. Just the thought of her being around me, made me want to be a better person. Over the last few months, I had done so many bad things, to so many people, that I had felt that I was the last person on earth that disserved to be happy. With all the turmoil and revenge that had been building within me, I had forgotten the true meaning of life, happiness. And somewhere along the way I had forgotten to "live life to the fullest" like my brother had taught me.

"You know you think too much," she said as she splashed water at me. "Hello! Hot girl in a bathing suit wants you to get in the water with her."

I might over think things sometimes, but I was not going to do it this time. 5.7 seconds, the amount of time it took me to get my shirt off, get in the water, and begin to splash back.

My mind allowed me to swim for about a half an hour, before it began to kick in again. My mind started to stress and I began to worry about what was going to happen. I knew for certain that like everything else in my life, all great things must come to an end. What would happen next? Would the bad things I had done in my past, scare Elizabeth off? After we crossed the line of our friendship, I knew there was no turning back. But did she know that? What was all this leading up to? Should I sacrifice the one friendship I wanted to keep, for a girlfriend?

"What now?" She asked.

"Do you ever think about the past?" I answered.

"Not really," she replied. "I like to live in the now."

"Well, there are some things I have done in my past. That I'm not particularly proud of and I just don't want to scare you . . ."

"I don't care about those things. I know who you are now. I'm not going anywhere," she said as she reached down and grabbed my hand. "Are you ready to get out?"

I instantly felt a shock as her hand touched mine. Like a few thousand volts coursing through my veins. My mind scrambled quickly, but not like it usually did. It was calming and shutting down. I had never felt so confused. It was as if I could not move, but at the same time I felt that I could move mountains. My heart felt that I could part the red sea, but I could not summon the energy to crawl out of the ocean. I did not know why, but for some odd reason I was having a lucky day. For when my body went limp from the somewhat electroshock I had received. At least, I had begun to float on my back. For if I had not. I probably would have drowned. I just laid there. Floating on top of the water and allowing the waves to carry me to the shore.

"That's pretty cool. How are you doing that?" Elizabeth asked.

"Doing what?"

"You're floating in, but the tide is going out?" She answered.

I did not have the slightest idea of why it was happening, so I did not even try to answer. As I got closer to the shore, I flipped over onto my stomach, and reached for the bottom. My arms felt weak and my legs began to tremble a little as I tried to stand up. I could not make it to my feet yet, so I just crawled out of the water. I looked like I was clawing my way onto the shores of Normandy. And acting like I was in search of my legs that had been blown off.

"Are you ok?" Elizabeth asked.

"Fine," I answered as my arms finally gave out and I rolled on to my back. Something was wrong. I did not know what but something very strange was happening to me and I could not explain it.

"Are you hurt? You're not bleeding or anything are you?" She asked.

"Only in my heart," I thought. I believe while I was out there fighting for my life, my heart had actually skipped a beat. "Smokers lungs," I said as I gasped for air. Was I dying? Maybe I was sick. I did not really know what was happening to me but it had to be something serious.

"You don't smoke . . ." She started to answer.

"Yea, I know . . . but my mother does," I answered quickly. "Second hand smoke, it's a killer."

"Oh," she replied as she began to lie down next to me.

She laid her head on my chest, wrapped my arm around her, and cradled my hand in hers. *"A perfect match,"* I thought as our fingers intertwined and locked together. I had spent an entire lifetime meeting people, but I had never felt that close to anyone in my life. Was I merely coming down with a cold or something? Or could it be that I had finally fallen in love?

Hoping for a comparison, I quickly remembered back to the day I asked Eddie what it was like to fall in love. I had assumed him and his long time girlfriend Maria were in love. Because, every time she called, before he hung up, she would say "I love you."

Eddie told me that there was no such thing as love. If anything, he showed me that he did not know how to love anyone. He would reply to her after her reaching out to him with, "I lust you too," and then hang up on her. But something about the way I felt made me believe that love was real. What else could explain it? What else could explain the repetitive heart beat still pounding, as if it were about to protrude from my chest cavity? And who could forget the strengthening weakness, I had encountered, that clouded my ability to even stand up?

It had been almost an hour since either of us had spoken a word. We were just resting there for a moment, watching the clouds pass by. I did not want to jinx it, by saying anything. Just my luck I would speak and my beautiful dream would come to an end.

"So about your psychic abilities," she said. "Did you know what was going to happen today? I'm only asking because I just wanted to make sure this isn't some sort of trick."

"I truthfully haven't known what's been going on for the last few hours now," I answered.

It had been strange. It kind of came and went as it pleased. At least that is what it had been doing for the last few hours now. I had not been able to think about anything but Elizabeth, for a while now. I honestly could have cared less if it ever came back.

"Good," she said. "That would have been really weird, if you had known exactly what to say, to make things like they are right now."

"I truthfully wouldn't want to cheapen the moments that I spend with you, by cheating," I answered. Where were these answers coming from? They were not of my own thought. Apparently, this woman had raddled me. I didn't even know what I was saying anymore. I mean 'I wouldn't want to cheapen the moments by cheating.' She had to be the one cheating. Maybe she was using some sort of mind trick or mind influence. She might as well have been answering her own questions.

"Do you always know exactly what to say?" She asked.

"Only when it comes to you," I said as I smiled. I could have fought with myself all night. But instead, I decided to give in, and allow whatever was going to happen, to happen. In the long run what could it really hurt? I mean other than giving in to the Goddesses powers and turning completely submissive to her every whim? Nothing could really go wrong with this approach. Honestly, I don't believe I could have fought it anymore anyway.

"I knew what you were thinking when you were mad at me," I said. I don't really know if I was saying it to defend myself from a possible heartbreak. Or if I was trying to clear the air by being completely honest, but it apparently it needed to be said so I could read her reaction. "You were upset about how it had happened and wondering if it could have been avoided. And no, it wasn't because of my psychic abilities."

"Then how did you know what I was thinking?" She asked.

"There are two possible scenarios that will play out when someone is mad at someone else for something they did. Take our disagreement for example. You could be mad at me for something I did wrong, which was fighting. If you believed I had done something wrong, you would ultimately feel the need to make me pay for my transgressions. The second scenario is that you would be mad at the circumstances of the fight. In which you agree with what I did, but disagree with me from an obsessive standpoint because it wasn't what you wanted to happen. Which would lead you to forgive me because you were never really mad at me," I answered.

"So you read my reaction to understand what I was thinking about subconsciously?" She replied.

"Yes," I said feeling slightly stunned as if she were reading my own mind. "That's exactly what I'm saying."

"Awesome, you learn something new everyday."

It didn't seem like it, but we had lied there on the ground for hours. The sun had begun to set and the stars were beginning to become more visible. The wind was calm and the moon shined just enough to see the white foam that rode in on top of the waves. A peaceful breeze picked up as I closed my eyes and embraced a deep calming breath. I had finally realized that it was times like these that made life worth living. Cuddled up on the ground with the person you love the most in this world. While you spend time staring at the sky, watching the moon, and hoping to see a shooting star. For a man, in those moments, you discover that you are enough. After moments of wondering if you will ever amount to anything in her eyes. Along with all of the other, "if" questions racing through your mind. You figure out that even if you do not feel you are what she desires. You will push and stride to be exactly what she needs. You may never be a millionaire, but you will provide for her. You will probably never discover the cure for cancer, but you will take care of her when she is ill. You are definitely not "Mr. Perfect," but you will always be a shoulder to cry on. In the end, when you discover these things about yourself. You will find out that is exactly what most women truly desire anyway. And you have let all of those "if" questions bother you for nothing. It is where the boy you are, and the man you could be; meet for the first time.

"Well do you want to wash off, before we head home?" She said as she stood up.

"Sure," I answered. As I stood, my legs were still a little shaky. So I slowly crept back down to the water. I was so nervous my knees were knocking together. After washing myself off, I quickly made my way to my truck. I slid myself into the seat, gently closed my eyes, and took a couple of deep breathes before Elizabeth got in. I could not believe what was happening to me. At that moment, I began to feel like my heart was about to explode. I couldn't get myself to calm down. I began to twitch and shiver, like a small Chihuahua. As if I was cold or something, but I was not. It was actually still kind of warm outside.

"Are you cold?" Elizabeth asked, as she climbed into the truck, noticing my nervous twitch.

"A little," I answered not wanting her to know I was nervous. My whole electrical system for warmth, and apparently the ability to have a clear thought, was shot.

"Well let's turn on some heat," she said scooting herself right next to me and turning the knob on the heater.

As we headed down the beach access road my shivers slowly went away, and I was beginning to calm down again. I began thinking about what had happened that day. How much would our relationship change? Was everything going to work out? I had never had an actual girlfriend before. Would I end up screwing everything up as usual? Just then, I remembered something Elizabeth had said earlier that day, about living in the now. After realizing she was right, I decided to put my arm around her. But instead of my arm going around her shoulder, I chickened out at the last second, and draped it over the back of the seat.

"Smooth one," she smiled.

"Oh! Great! You're an idiot!!!" I thought to myself, as she grabbed my hand and pulled it back around her. *"Denied,"* I continued to think to myself. I began to wonder if I had tried to move too quickly. As my mind finally stopped thinking, I felt her clasp my hand in between both of hers, and slip them in between her knees. She gently laid her head on my shoulder and closed her eyes. My mind began racing and my nervous shivers began to come back. Now trying to calm myself I decided to strike up a conversation. "So, which do you prefer, Eliza or Beth?"

"Well, everyone calls me Eliza, Lizzy, or Liz. Nobody really calls me Beth anymore . . ."

"I know . . ." I interrupted her. "Because that was what you're parents used to call you."

"How did you know . . . ? Oh yeah," She replied as she began to reposition herself as if to get closer to me.

"I don't mean to remind you of a terrible time in your life or anything by calling you Beth . . ."

"It's ok," she stopped me. "That time has come and gone. I kind of like it when you use it. I only think of the good times with my parents when you say it."

"Strange," I said to myself. It was the first time that I could recall, that I had influenced someone in a way that was not negative.

As I pulled into her driveway, she opened her eyes and looked up at me. I slowly moved in to kiss her good night, when I felt something unexpected, her pulse. It was racing. Not because of the passionate kiss we were about to share but because she was nervous and scared. I did not know for certain, until I saw her bottom lip quiver a bit. I had done the very same thing that Eddie had done to Maria. Elizabeth had reached out to me, by giving me a piece of herself. And what did I do? I gave her nothing in return. I had said nothing to let her know how I felt about her.

"Til' the end of day's!" I blurted. She then opened her eyes and her heart began to race even faster. She had known what the words meant, and I had frightened her.

"You don't mean that?" She answered now sitting back in the seat.

"No wait let me explain! I just meant that you reached out to me, letting me know how you felt. And I have said nearly nothing all day." I said trying to calm her, "I just wanted you to know that I'm not going anywhere either and I really like you too." With my hand still cradled in the both of hers, I instantly felt her heartbeat slow down, from the pulse in her wrist.

I again, leaned in for a kiss goodnight, and allowed myself to let go. I released my desires and ambitions in the world and allotted myself a moment of peace. As absent mindedness surrounded me, her unrelentingly effervescent lips touched mine. For a moment, I lost not only the resulting opinion of who I believed I was, but my position in subsistence as well. It had felt like another igniting spark had begun rushing through my veins. But this time it came from the outside in, towards my heart this time. The pulsating glint caused my heart to literally omit a single beat, and rejoin hers in what seemed like an unsullied duet.

"So I'll see you tomorrow?" She said with a whisper as she unimpeded me from her hypnotizing clutches.

"Ah . . . Ah . . ." I began to answer, before trying to refocus on what was going on. "I'll see you tomorrow," I continued as she stepped out of the vehicle and directed herself towards the front door.

My mind began conflicting with itself again, after I pulled out of the driveway. What happened to me today? What was this girl doing to me? She made me feel like I needed to alter everything I had ever known. At times she would leave me speechless and other times she would make me feel almost dense around her. And tonight did not seem to make things much easier. I had never felt so feeble and so completely out of control. It was like a type of guerilla warfare to rip me to shreds from the inside out, starting with the heart.

Chapter 18

The next day, I could barely keep my eyes open. I had stayed up all night, thinking about everything that had happened the day before. I just sat in the library, hoping and praying that I could catch a little shut eye before school started. My mind was running a little slow after not getting any sleep, and as for my foresight. I had not gone to sleep, so I did not receive anything. I could not help myself in any form or fashion. My mind could only focus on one thing at a time. It continually went over the same unnecessary things, which were redundant visions from the day before.

"Are you ok?" A voice said coming up from behind me.

"I'm ok," I answered as I turned around and saw Lynn walking up from behind.

"Well you look like crap!" She laughed.

"Thanks, can I help you with something?" I asked, as I fought to keep my bloodshot eyes open.

"Yea! First I just wanted to say thank you for what you did the other night."

"You're welcome," I answered.

"Truthfully, I was just hoping David would not find out about it, and do something stupid. Anyway, David called me last night, and we were talking about Elizabeth and yourself. Then we talked about our future . . ."

"Get to the point Lynn."

"Oh yea! He said to give you a message. 'It looks like something's about to go down.' Whatever that means?"

As complicated as it was, as Lynn walked away, my mind began suppressing much needed information. I knew that this day was going to come sooner or later. It just so happened to be the worst possible day. "Where's Beth?" I asked as I followed her to the door.

"You know, for you being her boyfriend. You really don't know anything about her," she answered. "She had homecoming committee this morning in the basketball gym."

As I ran out the door, I began to focus on the task at hand. I knew that I needed to get some sleep, so my brain would download the images of what was to come. But first, I had to check and make sure Elizabeth was going to be ok. I noticed the hallways were packed that morning, as I rushed as fast as I could towards the gym. I began pushing my way through packs of people, when I felt a hand grab my shoulder, and spin me around.

"Hey freak! I hear your seeing my girl," Luke said.

"Not now," I said as I began to take off again. As I turned around, the hand again, grabbed my shoulder.

"Not so fast," Luke barked.

"I'll break your nose later Luke . . ." I said as he took a swing at me.

I knew I did not have the time for this. I needed to get to Elizabeth and get out of the school. *"I cannot stand here and do this all day,"* I thought as I dodged his left jab and ducked his right hook. I instantly countered back by coming directly up with an upper cut. I could have stayed and made sure he was ok. But I had better things to do.

I quickly slowed down as I entered the main doors and noticed that the gym was nearly empty. As I rounded the corner, I caught a glimpse of her, and eventually slowed down entirely coming to a complete stop. She was out on the floor of the court, showing the other cheerleaders a new cheer. I never saw her look so happy. She was glowing with enthusiasm. I just stood there for a few moments thinking, *"What does she see in me? She's so beautiful, intelligent, and has the biggest heart I've ever seen."*

I let out a huge sigh as I turned around to exit the building. I had done what I had set out to do, by checking to see if she was ok, and she was fine. Now, I needed to try my best and make sure I did not drag her into my problems. There is a phrase coined for these types of situations, life is what you make it. But the secret to this phrase is very important. Life is exactly what you make it. If you want your life to be utter chaos, it will be chaotic. If you want it to be pleasant and enjoyable, than that is what it shall be. And if you want your life to be spent going from one drunken rampage to another, then that is exactly what it will be. Needless to say, I believed that I had made my choice a little too prematurely, for my life was about to change. Before my very eyes, my life would now alter. It would become chaotic and filled with an assortment of prior problematic associates.

"Will!" She said as she saw me turn around and head for the doors. As she ran to catch up with me, I quickly took a few deep breathes. "What's wrong?" She continued as she stepped closer and saw my bloodshot eyes.

"Nothing," I answered. "I have to take off for the day and I just wanted to see you before I left . . ."

"Why?" She replied.

I tried to think of many things to say, for an excuse, but nothing came to mind. I quickly thought about what Lynn had said and began to change the subject. "You told Lynn, that I was your boyfriend?"

"Don't start with me, William Joseph Larson," she replied. "What's really going on? If you don't tell me the truth, I'm not going to let you go."

You see this is the same predicament that I did not want to get into. Back at the diner when David needed my help and all Lynn would have had to say was do not go. And regardless of how important it was for David to leave, he would have stayed for her. I felt like I was about to have that same dilemma.

I thought for a moment about what she had said, and then grabbed her by the hand. We passed through the main doors and then out to the parking lot. I had come to the conclusion that she had come up with the better idea. Why not just take her with me? Then I would not have to worry about her at all.

"Where are we going?" She asked as we reached her car.

"You're just going to have to trust me," I answered. I could see the fear in her eyes and before long I knew I would need to start divulging my entire story. From where I had left off at the church, up to my vengeance that I would inevitably take later tonight. "Something's going to happen, I don't know what exactly. But until I find out, I need you to stay with me. Just follow me in your car to my house," I continued. "Please, just trust me and get into your car," I pleaded with her.

Chapter 19

We had just made it into the house, when I began to tell her what was happening. There was really no time to spare, so I began with the back story. After saving Anthony from being arrested, I began to hang out more frequently with him and Justin. Anytime anything came up that might be a little too dangerous or anything that nobody else wanted to do. I would stupidly volunteer myself for such tasks. I needed to gain their trust somehow. I did not have enough time to get into the specifics, but she got the idea.

One night, after drinking heavily, Justin asked me to break into the pawnshop just down the street. If I had not been drinking, I would have had my psychic foresight. And I would have known that it was owned by Justin's father.

When I finished picking the lock, of the pawnshop front door, I quietly began to open the door. As the door began to squeak open, Anthony grabbed the door knob, and flung it open. I stepped in to see Justin pointing a gun at me.

"What's your name?" Justin yelled as I shut the door behind me.

"Joe," I answered. I had given them my middle name so they would not realize who I was. Last names were not, for all intents and purposes, an imperative piece of information. Eddie and I never really looked too much alike anyway. I thought it would work, but apparently I was not fooling anyone.

"That's weird," Justin replied as he stepped closer. "I heard your name was Will . . . Will Larson."

When holding someone at gunpoint there are four vital mistakes that the shooter could make. Number one; is making sure you actually have ammunition. Two; is making sure you have cleaned your weapon properly. It could cause a misfire if it is not cleaned appropriately. Number three; always remember where the safety is located. The last piece of critical information that one must know when holding someone at gunpoint; is you must make sure you never get too close to the target. There was Justin's mistake. He got too close to me.

I reached behind me and grabbed the door knob with right hand, and closed my eyes as I heard him pull the hammer back on the firearm. I quickly, with the left hand, slapped the gun. When I did, it fired a round into the ceiling. I twisted the door handle from behind me and ran out the door, straight into a cop car. The officer jumped out of the car and yelled for me to freeze.

While he was taking statements from Anthony and Justin, I grabbed my tools that I had used to break into the pawn shop and tossed them into the gutter. Three weeks later I stood in front of a judge. I told her that they were my friends and they had asked me to meet them at the pawn shop. They had no evidence that I had broken in. So they had no choice, but to let me go. But before I got out of the court house, the judge stopped me. "I don't know exactly what happened at that pawn shop," she said. "But if they really are your friends. Apparently, they don't want to be friends with you anymore. And I don't really want to see you in my courtroom again."

I could understand why she was upset. I cannot help it that I can flip through the law book of Oklahoma and know more than some of the more seasoned lawyer's. And yes I did make most of them look like fools. But honestly whose fault was that? I thought for a moment about what she was saying and replied. "So you're asking me to leave?"

She looked at me sincerely and said, "No, I'm not asking, I'm down right demanding it. You have made a mockery of my courtroom for the last time Mr. Larson. I cannot make you go, but your father can. If need be I will tell him to take you elsewhere." Shortly thereafter, I moved here to Corpus.

"But wait," Elizabeth interrupted. "What does any of that have to do with you being here in Corpus and us having to leave school?"

"I'm getting to that." I continued. "Two weeks before I broke into the pawnshop. I heard Justin's cell phone ring. When I picked it up to hand it to him, I glanced at the phone number. The number was a number I had never seen before, but my eidetic memory stored it for me and would not allow me to forget. When he hung up the phone, I asked him who it was. He complied telling me it was his cousin.

After I got out of trouble and spoke to the judge. My father asked me where I wanted to make our new home. I went to the library and searched the records. I was hunting for area codes and prefixes. I later found out that the number was a Corpus Christi number."

"So his cousin lives here?" She asked. "Do you know who it is?"

As I was about to answer her, my cell phone rang. "Hello," I said.

"Will," the voice answered back. "How ya doin', I been keepin' a eye ouwt fur ya."

"I know who this is, Matt," I replied. I could hear the faint sound of his jaw cracking and popping in the background.

"Good, then we don have to play da guessin' game," he answered. "Mee me at da beach at ten tonight."

"And if I don't . . ."

"Let's jus say, if I go ta da beach and you're not there," he muttered. "I'm gonna make a liddle trip ta your girlfriends' house. And have a visit wid da family," he answered just before the line went dead.

"Who was that?" Elizabeth asked.

"Justin's cousin," I answered.

"I don't get it, why move to where he had relatives?"

"I still wanted to know why? Why did they kill my brother?"

"So, what do we do next?"

"I need to get some sleep," I said as I made my way to my room.

I decided to lie in my bed for a moment. I was running everything through my mind, as I began trying to piece everything together. I had to meet Matt at the beach at 10:00 PM. I had wondered for the longest time if this day would ever come; the day that I would avenge my brother. Now as I lay in my bed, I didn't know if I wanted to go through with it. Of course I was angry and wanted to end things. But everything had changed in the last couple of weeks. Just by being around Elizabeth, I had felt happier than I had ever deserved.

"Hey Lynn," I heard Elizabeth talking on the phone with her cousin. "Just tell my teachers that I was sick and had to stay home for the day." She continued. "Thanks Lynn."

I had forgotten completely about the fact that Elizabeth could have been in trouble for leaving school. But I just wanted to make sure she was safe. Who was I to screw up her life just because I was a selfish prick?

"I was sure you wouldn't be asleep yet," she said as she entered the room. She began to lie down next to me and cuddled up to me as close as she could. She then grabbed my arm, and draped it over her. With her staring directly into my eye's she asked, "Why must you do this?"

"I don't know anymore," I answered. None of it had really seemed all that important anymore. Now I didn't even know if I could actually pull the trigger. I might have changed too much in the last couple of weeks. But I found my reason to follow through with it when she asked, "Then why do it at all?"

"I have to now," I replied. "I took it too far and these guys don't play by the rules. If I don't meet up with them tonight, something bad could happen. To you, your family, or even my own. And I won't let that happen. Everything's going to be ok," I continued. "You just have to trust me."

"I do Will," she answered. "I just don't want anything to happen to you."

It didn't take long for me to begin to fade into unconsciousness. As a grogginess of immense proportions swept over my psychological status, I felt Elizabeth move in closer to me. As I drifted into a deep slumber, I heard a voice say, "I love you." I then felt Elizabeth flip over and spoon up close to me.

I held her as tightly as I possibly could and replied, "I love you too!"

Chapter 20

Still in my bed, I awoke just a few hours later, well rested. It was noon and Elizabeth had left the room. My mind instantly stopped downloading as I ran out of the room to look for her. When I opened the door, I saw her sitting on the couch. She was just sitting there, holding her knees with her arms and staring out the window. Something had changed. One of those deeply concerning questions that I had bothered myself with must have came true.

"What's wrong?" I asked as I sat down next to her and wiped the sleep from my eyes. Although I was hoping it was something I could fix. I prepared for the worst.

"Um . . . You know that you told me that you loved me, right?" She replied with a confused look.

"Oh, is that all," I said as I smiled. "I realize that it seemed a little early, to be saying it. But, like in the story I told you about my great-grandfather. In my family, love means that I couldn't live without you. I mean I'm not really much of a people person. I don't have any friends, and I don't really have all that much family either. At times I feel like I'm all alone in the world and I truly hate feeling that way. It took me seventeen years, ten months, and twenty-one days to find you. Not only are you beautiful, confident, and deceivingly intelligent. But for some odd reason you seem to be interested in me, which for the life of me I cannot understand."

"Oh," she said as she began to smile. After thinking for a moment about what I had been saying she replied, "In that case, I love you too!"

"Wait," I stopped for a moment. "I only said it because you said it to me first," I continued as I began to think back to what had happened before I had fallen asleep. "I didn't want to leave you hanging, yet again, after you had reached out to me."

"But," she answered with that same confused look from before. "I didn't say it to you?"

I began to feel very confused. I was sure she told me that she loved me. Was I hearing things? Was I losing my mind? I could not really be sure of anything anymore. I was coming to the conclusion that my mind was shot. It was either that or maybe I was still a little delirious from not getting any sleep from the night before? It no longer mattered whichever direction my mind was beginning to head. The point was that my mental capabilities were utterly useless to me now.

"It's ok," Elizabeth said interrupting the battle of whits I was having with myself. "I said it back to you now. That's all that matters, right? And I truthfully couldn't see myself spending a day without you either."

"Are you reading my thoughts, Ms. Trujillo?" I asked.

"I don't have to, I just know you that well," she answered.

I had wished now, that I had not rushed out of the bedroom, after awaking. But because I had rushed out, I had only received about half of the images I so desperately needed. I had no earthly idea of what was to come, but I was confident nonetheless. I had to be, for Elizabeth's sake. My only fear was that my senses would eventually give out on me. But I couldn't think that way. Everything would be fine. I definitely knew that I could not show Elizabeth that I was stressing about anything. The last thing I needed was to terrify her and make it to where she would ask me to stay. I knew that I needed to finish what I had started. I could have forgiven them for what they had done, but if I did not end it tonight, they would just continue to track me down. The people I loved would never be safe.

"So how did you know Matt was Justin's cousin?" Elizabeth asked.

"In theory, an eidetic memory is an absolutely flawless quality," I said. "But that is only in theory. If you add alcohol or drugs to the equation, your mind may begin to fog over and confuse you even more. I knew for sure that the number came from a Corpus phone, but I could not remember the whole number. I tried for days to see it in my mind when I tried to recall it, but the harder I tried, the more mixed up I would become. Before long I started second guessing myself and thinking that I had not seen the number all that well. Not long after that, confused and dismayed, I began to assume that I never saw the number at all. Maybe it was nothing more than a figment of my own imagination and I had moved to Corpus for nothing. But after my first day here, I met Matt, and he seemed very familiar. But yet again I was drunk when I met him. So I was not for sure, until I met him at the convenient store. He was so doped up. I heard almost every thought he had. He basically told me himself, without actually saying anything."

"So, what do we do now?" She asked.

I was still very uncertain, of whether or not to tell her that I had no idea. Nothing I had seen so far, had yet clicked my abilities, but this could be a good sign. That could mean that my visions would not click on, until later that evening. So I began to feel a little comfortable about the situation, almost like I was beginning to like my chances of making it through the night alive.

"For now we wait . . ." I stopped as I heard a vehicle pull in the drive way. "Someone's here!" I looked out the window and saw my father stepping out of his truck. "It's my dad."

"Should I go hide?" Elizabeth asked.

Getting caught skipping school was not really part of my plan. If he found out I missed another day of school for no reason. I could only imagine his angered life lesson speech that he might come up with. But as his door on his truck shut, something clicked in my head. I did not really want my visions to come back to me so early, but I could not complain. It was about to save me from having a heated argument between my father and I. "No, he's going to spend a few minutes putting tools in the garage, which will give us plenty of time. There is a can of soup in the cabinet, next to the stove. Open it, put it in a bowl, and put it in the microwave for two minutes." I answered. "When it's done meet me in the bedroom."

As she rushed towards the kitchen, I ran into my bedroom. Looks can be deceiving and I needed to look sick. I began donning on every sweater and jacket I could find. After slipping on 4 sweaters and 2 coats,

I began running around the room. I was hoping my smoker's cough, from my mother smoking around me, would come back. As Elizabeth entered the room I gave her instructions on what to do. I quickly jumped into bed and covered myself up to my head.

"Will?" My father said as he entered the house. "Are you here?"

"Back here dad," I coughed.

"What's going on?" He asked as he walked into the room.

"Well I should get back to school," Elizabeth said as she stepped out of the room.

My father looked angry as he stepped closer to my bed, but the anger quickly faded. As he stepped closer he saw my pasty colorless and sweaty face, along with the bowl of soup next to my bed. "Are you ok?" He asked.

"I'll be fine, I think it's just a cold," I answered out of breath. As I spoke the words, my visions fled from my mind. "Beth just came by during her lunch hour, to bring me a bowl of soup."

"Well that was pretty nice of her," he replied. "You better not let that one go," he said as we heard the front door shut behind Elizabeth.

"I'll try not to," I answered.

"I'll be out here eating lunch if you need anything," he said. "Oh yea!" He continued. I was sure I had just been caught and began to freak out a little bit. "I have something to take care of after work. So I won't be home until late tonight."

"Ok," I said as he walked out the door. I waited for thirty minutes, under a blanket with 7 layers of clothing on, for him to leave. I did not want to lie to my father, but I had no choice. I quickly rushed to the shower, stripped my clothes off, and began to cool off under the cool water.

After a few minutes in the shower, I stepped out, and heard the door shut. "Will?" Elizabeth said.

"I'm in the bathroom," I replied as I got dressed. I knew I had to do something right, before my visions would come back. I was not really looking forward to waiting for the last possible second either. So I exited the bathroom and sat down on the couch next to Elizabeth. I looked into her eyes and said, "I love you." Without hesitation images began flooding back in. My mind reallocated and had an aching twinge as usual, as my vision again began to fade into complete darkness.

I awoke with my head in Elizabeth's lap as she replied, "I love you too." She had sat there the whole time, looking after me, and continuously running her fingers through my hair. "I think I might actually, be getting used to this. At least you passing out all the time," She added as she leaned down and kissed me. I instantly thought back to my definition of the word love. I could not even envision living another second without this woman, little alone imagine a whole day.

"How long have I been out," I asked as she looked over to the clock.

"Four hours and 13 minutes, its 5:00 PM on the dot," she answered. "Did you receive any new images?"

"No," I said. I still could not believe that I had been unconscious for 4 hours. It had never done anything like that before. *"I must have just been tired,"* I thought to myself.

"What time are you going to take me home?" Elizabeth asked.

"I'm not," I answered.

She seemed worried, like she was just asking random questions. She was trying her best to stray away from the ultimate question, *"you're not going to die tonight are you?"* I had sensed it a couple of times. I could almost see it rolling off of the tip of her tongue at any moment.

"I'm going to be fine," I told her trying to sooth her thoughts. I did not know for sure what was going to happen tonight, but she did not need to stress out. I knew I was going to have to spend the rest of my time with her that night. And I did not want to have to spend it trying to explain to her what I had thought was going to happen. I was very important that I tried to stay away from trying to lie to her. For it would not have done either of us any good.

"So, we have plenty of time now. Why don't you tell me about her?" She asked. I did not know exactly who she was referring to, so I stayed quiet until she asked. "Tell me about Cheyenne?"

"Well, it's in Wyoming," I joked. I knew now what she was talking about. She wanted to know about my fake girlfriend. I didn't have the slightest idea of what I was going to do. I didn't need to lie to her but telling the truth could have its own consequences.

"No, really Will. I want to know what she was like. She was your last girlfriend and it might be detrimental to our relationship surviving."

"She's a brunette," I blurted. I did not know why I was trying so hard to give details of a girl that did not exist. But I was not really being completely dishonest. When I was a kid, I did meet a girl named Cheyenne, and she was a brunette. "She has blue eyes . . . I mean . . . brown eyes," I said as she shot me a strange look for changing my answer in mid-sentence. But I had forgotten my father's key elements to describing a girl/woman. Do not get me wrong, my father is not some sort of sleaze bag. But when describing another woman to my mother he uses this method. It is his way of choosing his battle's wisely. Why fight over something that does not matter? But using the wrong words in this type of situation will inevitably end in a fight and for me an unconscious slumber. But I had an idea of what to do. If I just thought about the question and categorized it about someone I already knew. I might be able to make it out of the conversation without the deeply painful nap. I was still telling the truth with just bending it a little.

When using my father's techniques there are a few things to keep in mind. When you are describing another girl/woman, to the woman you love. Never make the girl sound prettier, smarter, or more slender. The girl you describe must seem like any other girl/woman, and is, and always will be less remarkable than the one you love. "She's alright looking," I continued thinking about the real Cheyenne. With saying something like: she's alright looking, or pointing out physical flaws like freckles or a mole; not only is it vague, which is exactly what you want, but it also makes you sound shallow. So it is best to follow it up with something positive. "But she has a big heart and she likes me for me," I said thinking about Elizabeth. By saying she likes me for me, it works for my predicament. But if you are talking to your girlfriend about another girl you met on the street. You might want to say something like: she had a kind smile or she seemed nice. Stray away from describing her down to the smallest of details. Because then you sound like you paid too much attention. Keep in mind, the less you say, the better it is for you in the long run.

"So what does she do for fun?" She asked.

"Well, on the weekends she likes to burn puppies at the stake," I laughed. Humor is another helping hand. When on the spot and you do not know what to say. Say something stupid and hope she laughs hard enough to forget what you are talking about in the first place. Not only does it keep the conversation light, it also usually does not anger too many people. But it also gives you enough time, to think of something, to answer the question.

"Alright," she laughed. "Now really . . ."

"I don't know, the same things we like to do," I answered thinking about the real Cheyenne. Remember to keep things vague, when they are trying to paint a picture in their minds. Do not think like De Vinci, you know a clear and perfect picture. Think Picasso, sort of blurred and pieced together.

"So what do you love about her?" She asked.

Last but not least, the final test. Love is an entrapment word. Never, under any circumstances, do you ever use the word love. You did not love her hair, her eye color, or her dress. Even when answering a question like this, switch out the word love. Either switch it out with the word like or do not use either word at all. "She always seems to be there when I need her," I answered now thinking of Elizabeth again.

My new theory of categorizing her questions and mixing them with my father's methods was working beautifully. I was beginning to believe what with a little luck on my side, I might be able to survive our intricate conversations.

Chapter 21

8:32 the clock read, as I rolled off the couch on to the floor. "Are you about ready to go?" I asked her.

"Where to?" She said.

I knew I could not take her home. I could not really see Anthony or Justin hurting her or anyone in her family. But if they had Elizabeth, they would have leverage over me. She was the only person in the world that I cared for anymore. And there was no way I was going to let anything happen to her. "I'm going to take you to David's house," I said. He was the only person I believed I could trust with this type of emergency and with present company excluded, the only friend I had.

"And what are you going to do?" She asked.

I had planned on going to the beach and getting prepared. I knew it would take at least ten minutes, or so, for my mind to get used to everything, again. That and I wanted to check out the area where we were going to meet. One must know one's own territory before going to war. "I'm going to go to the beach to scope everything out."

"Why don't you just take me with you?"

"That is completely out of the question," I answered.

As we walked out the door towards my truck, I began praying that Justin and Anthony would not stoop so low as to bringing Elizabeth into our quarrel. Matt knew of every place she could possibly be. "Why not just take her with me?" I asked myself. She would probably be safer with me, but I did not want to take the chance.

I quickly fired my truck up and slipped it into drive. As I slowly slipped off the brake pedal, my visions began rushing in again. Not in full force, but just enough to give me a brief idea of what was to come. I now knew a little more of what was going to happen and more importantly, what I would need for battle.

"What's wrong?" Elizabeth asked as I slammed the truck into park.

"Nothing," I answered. "I just need to get some supplies from the garage."

My visions had been clear. Elizabeth would be fine at David's house. Justin, Anthony, and Matt would eventually leave her out of it and somehow I would survive the altercation. I just needed to keep a clear head and not divulge too much information. I now had a plan. If it was carried out, exactly like I had seen it in my mind, everything should be fine.

After tossing the supplies into the back of my truck, I hopped back into the front seat. "So this may or may not be the last time I see you?" Elizabeth asked.

I was very content with what I saw in my visions, but there were still hole's in what I saw. I did not want to discourage her with incomplete visions. So I stayed away from the subject. "Everything's going to be fine," I answered.

I parked in David's driveway and stepped out of my truck. The night sky was gloomy. The immense obscurity that was the night sky was loaded with an abundance of shade from the prolific storm brewing and progressively moving inland. As the ocean of clouds over head prepared to make my night a little more complicated. The lights instantly began to flick on in the house, followed by the front door opening, and David's shadow emerging.

"Who's there?" David asked.

"It's me! Will!" I answered back. "I need a favor."

"Consider it already done man, whatever you need." He said as we finally made it up the driveway to the front door.

I started by telling David what was going on with Anthony, Justin, and Matt. As I came to a close, I asked him the favor. "Can Beth stay here?"

"Of course man, you don't even have to ask. You don't need anything else do you?" He asked.

"No," I said as I showed him the gun tucked into my waist. "But if they come by here, shoot first, and ask questions later."

"I have a shot gun if you need it . . ." David stopped.

"What are you guys talking about?" Lynn asked as she walked out of the house.

As David changed the subject in mid sentence, she no longer desired to know about the conversation. "Yes that's all true," he continued. "But you have to understand my point of view. When nothing else seems to be working, this method will work 100% of the time. When you begin your task of trying to molest a goat or a sheep, you want to remember to wear the big rubber boots or cowboy boots. First, you don on the boots, and then you can stick their hind legs in them with you. I'm telling you it makes it much harder for them to get away!"

I could not help myself but to laugh a little as I regrettably asked, "What is it with you and farm animals?"

"I think I just told you the answer to that," he said as he himself began to breakdown and lose control of his own laughter.

Shortly thereafter, I said my goodbyes to Elizabeth. As I began to head for the beach, my mind was completely focused on what I had to accomplish. I had a few tricks up my sleeves and I just needed to arrive at the war zone before everyone else.

As I headed away from David's house, I quickly remembered why I hated coming over. He lived right next to the school and I hated hitting all of the speed bumps. Unfortunately, after trying so hard to stay focused on the task at hand. My mind steadily strayed from the essential and I began thinking about Elizabeth. How much she had changed me and what my life was like before I met her. I couldn't help it, before her, my life seemed like it was stuck on pause. It was a tenacious, yet lonesome disarray of an existence. The type of loneliness one feels, even when they are surrounded by people, but you still feel like something is missing: Much like a beautiful painting. There is always one key element to all masters of art. The painting may contain a smile, a flower, or death. No matter the elements surrounding it for they are obsolete. But without it, it would no longer stand out. It would just be another random painting. But that key element is necessary for it to become stunning, and allows the painting to be different. It is intended to make the work of art greater with it, rather than without it.

"If this was my last day on earth, would I go to Heaven or Hell?" I thought as my troubled mind began to ramble. If I went to Heaven, what would it be like? If I had the opportunity to go to Heaven, and I got to live one day over again; what would it be? That question was simpler than I had assumed. I would live my day down at the beach, with Elizabeth again. "Please Lord," I prayed, "let me live that day over and over again." On the plus side, if I did die and go to Heaven, perhaps I might also get a chance to see Eddie.

After pulling onto the beach from the access road, I parked a few yards away from where the festivities were about to take place. My father would never understand if I put a bullet hole in my truck. As I slid the truck into park, I bowed my head to pray. "Dear Lord, I know this is not what you had in mind for my life, but I need your help. I do not ask for a steady hand to kill my assailants or the opportunity for vengeance without life threatening ailments. I only ask if there is some kind of way I could get out of this predicament without killing anyone or dying myself. It would be greatly appreciated, but if not. Please forgive me for the poor unfortunate souls I am about to send your way. In Jesus name I pray, Amen." I then stepped out of my truck and reached in the back to get my bag of supplies. "I moved them over to the other side," Elizabeth said.

"Ah!!!!" I screamed. "What are you doing back there?!?"

Apparently, she had jumped in to the back of the truck when I was driving over the speed bumps. I felt happy that she loved me so much, but I had hoped she would have stayed at David's. "What's wrong with you?" I barked at her. "Why didn't you stay at David's?"

"I couldn't let you do this by yourself," she answered. "It's me and you William. We should take care of this together. I can help and I promise not to get in the way."

"This is not a walk in the park," I snapped at her. "People can and will most likely be dying tonight . . ." I stopped. I did not really have the time to stand here and fight with her. But I needed to think this through. I knew how I was supposed to get out of this. But now I had to make a plan for two people. Everything would have been fine, if she would have just stayed where she was.

"Are you going to think about it all night? Or are we going to do this?" She asked.

"Fine," I said as I grabbed my bag. It was not like I actually had a choice in the situation anymore.

As we headed towards the sand dunes, I tried my best to think of a way for Elizabeth to get out of here. *"If I died,"* I thought. *"That would be ok. I have come to terms with my maker and I am aware that I may not survive the altercation. But if something happened to Elizabeth?"* I quickly stressed my mind to stay away from even thinking about something that horrifying.

"Focus," I told myself. I could not see everything that was going to happen, but I could see where everyone was going to be standing. My supplies consisted of two bear traps, and a hand gun with four bullets. Usually coming from the country, you should know how to do at least two things. Foremost above all else is obtaining the knowledge it would take to fire a weapon at least decently accurate. The second is acquiring the consistency it takes to properly set a trap. Be it a raccoon, rabbit, coyote, or bear.

I had Elizabeth dig a couple of holes where Justin and Matt would end up standing. I wanted Anthony all to myself. I would kill him with my bare hands if need be. I hated Justin for shooting at me, and for giving Anthony the go ahead to take Eddie's life. But I had to avenge my brother and kill the man that took him from me. Anthony was the driver of the car that ran him off the road. So he would be the one I would seek my retribution from.

"Is the last trap set?" Elizabeth asked.

"Yes," I answered. "As much as I know you want to stay out here. You have to leave. Head down the beach to my truck," I told her. "As soon as you hear the first shot fire off, call the police, and take off."

"I don't want to leave you," she said.

"You have to," I replied. "I can't stay and finish this, unless you leave." I stopped for a moment waiting for a reaction but there was none. I knew now that I would have to make her leave. "Fine," I said as I attempted to change my approach. I was beginning to become angry. "What do I have to say to get you to head down the beach? It won't do me any good to lie to you. I can't tell you everything will be alright, when I honestly don't know. Just tell me what I need to say and I'll say it."

"I can help . . ." She started.

"Just stop!" I screamed at her. "Stop treating this like it's some sort of game. My life isn't filled with rainbows and butterflies like yours. It is filled with countless deaths of loved ones and a constant reasoning for hating humanity as a whole. Lives are on the line, people are going to die tonight, and I could be one of them. I will not allow you to be the next martyr in my life . . ." I stopped for a moment. *"What do you mean 'next martyr,'"* I thought to myself. *"Eddie died from his own actions, didn't he?"*

"Ok," she replied. "I'm going."

"It's a little too late for that!" I heard a voice from the past say.

"Stay behind me," I told her as I turned around to see Justin walk up the other side of the dunes.

Chapter 22

"You're early, what did you miss me?" I said as I pointed my weapon at Justin's head. "Where's the other two idiots'?" I asked as I stepped firmly in front of Elizabeth, and positioned her directly behind me with my free arm. I was pretty sure that I had plenty of time to get her out of here, but I was wrong. If I would have known she was going to stay, I would have brought more than a six shooter.

"They'll be here momentarily," he answered.

"Why did you do it?" I asked. "I have to know, why did you kill my brother?"

"You don't steal from us," he barked. "You should know that!"

"Why would Eddie want to take anything from you?" I yelled back at him.

"What are you talking about?" He asked. "Your brother was a bystander. Of course, it would have been nice if both of you had died in the accident. But if you would have just died like you were supposed to, none of us would be here."

Quickly a rush of visions infected my mind as I began to remember the true events of that night. Painful thoughts of my own actions were the cause of my brother's death as I saw myself in his car that fateful night. "Eddie, scoot over and let me drive."

"Ok," Eddie answered. "What's in the bag?"

"A way for us to pay for a better apartment," I answered as I peeled out heading out of town.

"Is that what I think it is? You know how I feel about drugs," he explained. "I thought you and Ben was going to stop . . ." He stopped for a moment as he closed his eyes.

"What was it?" I asked. "You just had a vision. What was it about?"

"Will, I know you don't understand this but today is the day you grow up . . ." He continued as I saw Anthony's car turn a corner and creep up behind us. "This is not the path your life is supposed to be on. Your lesson will be a hard one and not easily overcome, but you must be stopped, and I know now I must be the one to stop you."

"What are you talking about?" I asked as I felt Anthony's car nudge us from behind.

"Finish what you started and I'll meet you in the end, I promise. I do this out of love little bro'," he said as he grabbed the steering wheel and jerked, leading us to spin off the road into a tree.

My visions stopped as I saw Anthony and Matt walking up to meet Justin on the top of the dune. A swallow of disgust pushed my heart into my stomach. Like a tidal wave of weakness, with every beat through my extremities, I fought with myself just to keep the weapon around shoulder height. Shaken with my self esteem at an all time low, the time to strike was coming, and I needed to focus on the task at hand. Trying to find a new sense of courage, I felt that I deserved to die tonight, but I still needed to get Elizabeth off the beach. "I know that I did you wrong," I said to Justin. "But she has nothing to do with this. Just let her go and you can do whatever you want with me."

"Ah, sorry Will," he answered. "You know how I hate witnesses."

There would be time for remorse later. Like Eddie said, I needed to finish what I started. *"Wait for it,"* I told myself. *"As soon as Matt steps on the trap you need to fire."*

I focused as much as I could to aim up at the sand dunes towards Justin. I knew the coyote trap, would injure him. But it would not stop him from retaliating and firing a couple rounds at me. "Crack!" The coyote trap snapped Matt's ankle like a twig.

As Justin turned back to look at what had happened, "Whack!" The bear trap wrapped around Justin's leg. As the teeth of the trap dug into Justin's flesh, he turned back towards me. I had my shot and I took it, "Boom!" My gun fired a round, and struck Justin, just between the eyes. I quickly swung to the right, and "Boom!" I fired again. This one struck Matt in the chest.

As I began to turn my attention towards Anthony, "Boom!" Another gun had fired.

I felt a slight pain in my chest as the bullet skimmed off the left side of my rib cage. I quickly turned to see where the bullet had gone. When I did, I heard Elizabeth beginning to gasp for air. It was buried deep in her chest. When I turned back to the dunes, I only had one feeling, anger. I charged as fast as I could towards Anthony, not really caring about anything. I heard the gun fire a couple more time's as I reached the base of the mound. I felt like a bull that saw red. Pushing to reach the top of the knoll, fear and pain were now a nonfactor as I bulldogged him into the bottom of the dunes.

After hitting bottom, I climbed on top of him, and straddled his stomach. Now deeply deranged, the ability to contain my rage from overflow had become unfeasible. Elizabeth was hurt. That meant everyone had to die, even myself included if need be. I began striking him as hard as I possibly could. It wasn't my best fighting skills, but I could care less at the time. I was too busy trying to crack his head open like a walnut. Moments of blind rage are an unattractive site. You don't care about technique or even trying to scheme up a method. You only care about one thing. Barbarically tearing something to shreds and killing anyone that stands in your way.

As he went silent and his body had finally gone lifeless. I stood up and immediately felt an immense pain and a little faint. I instantly grabbed my stomach as the adrenaline slowly stopped pumping. When I looked down at my hands they were coated with blood. I had been shot two more times, while charging at Anthony. Once in the arm and the other struck me in the stomach. Still a little woozy, I regained some focus, and ran back over the dune. I had to get to Elizabeth. As I reached my destination, I fell down next to her, and sat her head in my lap. I wanted to tell her I was sorry. I wanted to say that I loved her, and let her know that everything was going to be ok. But I was too late. She was already gone.

Chapter 23

"Why?!?" I screamed as my mind and eyes began to fade into darkness. Why did Elizabeth have to die? I had tried so hard to keep her away from the predicament that I had put myself into. Why not me? I could never forgive myself for the things that I have done. *"Please Lord let me die as well,"* I prayed.

"Calm down Will," a familiar voice echoed.

As a nearly blinding light beamed in from nowhere, I instantly recognized the voice and complied, "Eddie? Is that you?" I had accepted the fact and presumed that I would never hear his voice again. Without Eddie, the last few months had been strange to say the least. But his clear and calm voice brought warmth to my soullessness. My emotional rollercoaster of a life had come to a sudden halt. I felt a moment of serenity from just hearing those three words of, *"Calm down Will."*

"Eddie? What's going on?" I continued. As my eyes began to focus and I saw his face. I could no longer control the emotional breakdown that I had been holding back for so long.

At first I tried to make myself believe it was him. I struggled with myself for a moment and assumed it was nothing more than a mirage. Until I heard him say, "Hey, little bro', you have to calm down. If you don't, you will die."

"It was like you said, 'I needed to finish what I started and you would meet me in the end.'"

"This isn't the end," Eddie laughed. "This is merely the beginning."

I had so many questions I wanted to ask him, but I could only think of one that seemed important at the time. "Is Beth Ok?"

131

"She's fine," he replied as I let out a sigh of relief.

I began by trying to explain to Eddie about what had happened while he was gone. How I had opened up to Elizabeth and how the trouble had eventually led to her death. Eddie did not seem to care about the trouble all that much. He seemed to care more about Elizabeth. Who she was? What kind of things we had in common? And whether or not she made me happy? I stopped for a moment as I realized that he did not really give me a direct answer about Elizabeth. He just said that she was fine. I was guessing when I thought it meant that she was in Heaven. Much like Eddie I had assumed the both of them would end up in Heaven for all the great things they did. And I would most likely end up in Hell, for all the trouble I had caused. With keeping all of that in mind, I stopped his questions, and began asking my own. "She'll be in a new place up there and most likely scared. Just do me a favor and keep an eye out for her . . ."

"Oh, I'll definitely keep an eye out for her. But Will," He stopped me. "She's not dead!"

His answer gave me peace of mind. It was short lived though, I had remembered back at the beach, her lifeless body in my arms. *"Good,"* I thought, *"maybe she'll live and I'll go in her place. But I will be headed in the other direction, but that's ok."*

"No," Eddie said, as he read my mind and tried to calm my thoughts.

"No what?" I asked. "Is she dying?"

"No! I've been trying my best, to send you some sort of signal," he replied. "Just shut your mouth and open your mind. I'll show you everything you need to know."

I had forgotten that Eddie and I could communicate through our thoughts. It was like our minds were tuned into the same station or running on the same frequency so to speak.

As soon as the visions began, everything in my mind began to click. Of course I knew that I was in the car with him when we wrecked. But now, Eddie and I were in comas at the Hospital. Eddie had been injured, but not as badly as I had. He had exhausted himself, using all of his extra energy, trying to break through to me.

In the first meeting at the church that I had with Elizabeth, she asked me, "Can you see everything?" But just before that, I was almost certain she had said, "Can you save him?" I was not hearing things. It was a nurse in the room talking to a doctor. Again another clue was in the greyhound race. The dog's name was, "tsi-li-hu yo-na." Eddie was calling me sleeping bear and trying to let me know that something was wrong. He was trying to convince me that I was asleep and I needed to wake up. And again when I thought I heard Elizabeth say she loved me. Just before I had fallen asleep, when we were together in my bed and I assumed I was delirious. It was actually a late night, in which my mother had spent with me. She was saying her goodbyes.

"Eddie I'm so sorry!" I cried out as tears filled my eyes and began to trickle down my face.

"It's ok," he said with a tear strolling down his own. "I'd do it again in a heartbeat to help you, little bro'."

"What about the fore sight, I had been receiving in my dreams? Was I just not getting them? Or is it gone now? Have I lost the S.S.T.S.T. as well?"

"Your brain has been lapsing for the last week and a half now," Eddie answered. "You still have the gifts God gave you. You just haven't been able to use them."

As I began to think about my time in Corpus I asked, "So when I was at the beach with Beth? When her hand touched mine, I had felt a shot of electricity. The doctors must have been trying to resuscitate me?"

"No," he chuckled. "Everything you felt for Eliza, was real,"

"So what was real and what wasn't?"

"You'll have to find out for yourself," he replied. "I can't answer all of your questions."

"What about the dream with Beth, holding my son?"

"Those weren't sent by me," he said as I looked at him puzzled. "Those images were sent by the almighty. They were sent to remind you of how great things can be, just by leading the right life."

"Ok so what next?" I asked assuming Eddie would be coming back with me. "Do we just wake up or what?"

"Not quite," he said with a long sigh. "That was how I was able to stop everything. They pulled my plug about five minutes ago." Struck by guilt my mind began to fill with an abyss of shame. Before I had a chance for a rebuttal Eddie interrupted my thoughts. "They pulled my plug first, you know what that means. I was harder to let go. You on the other hand would be like unplugging the toaster. You know because mom and dad don't love you."

"Shut up Eddie," I said as I laughed.

"Look, I won't ask you to go back. You know I would never make you do anything you didn't want to do. But before you make your decision, I have something for you to see," he answered. "Hey," he continued. "I know you don't realize it yet, but you will decide to go back. They will need you more now, than they ever have. I won't elaborate anymore than that, but please keep in mind. When you do go back, that God gave both of us some pretty awesome gifts, stop abusing yours," he said as he stepped back towards the blinding light. He stopped for a moment, looked back, smiled, and signed off for one last time. "I'll see you later little bro' . . . hopefully, much later."

Chapter 24

The images, in which Eddie had spoken of, began to submerge themselves into my mind, in full force. They were of things to come. The first was of our parents. After our wreck, they could not handle seeing each other every day. So they eventually split up completely. They even moved to separate states, to insure that they would never see each other again.

The next image was about Lynn and David. Lynn would spend the rest of her life, working two jobs, and would eventually follow in her mother's footsteps. While her husband David, would spend most of his time behind bars for petty crimes he committed. *"If I don't move to Texas and scare him away from his criminal life. This will ultimately be what happens?"* I asked myself.

The images following those brought an excess of chills down my spine. It was the dream that God had given me. I was in the bed, as usual. When I heard the scream, I stood up, and felt myself stagger a little. I assumed I must have been drunk. I quickly stumbled out of the room and down the hallway. The green construction paper, with Eddie's name on it was gone. As I opened the door, I noticed that it was not quite like it was before.

Elizabeth was sitting in the rocking chair, trying her best to put the child back to sleep. As she looked up at me an overabundance of sympathetic tears streamed from her bruised and distended eyes. "Stay away from my son!" She demanded. My eyes focused on her as my mind raged in anger. My hand swung wildly as it connected with her swollen and battered face. I quickly snapped back into control of myself. *"What is going on?"* I screamed at myself as my soul began to scrape and claw for some sort of deliverance. I quickly closed my eyes and began wishing the images would stop. When my eyes reopened, I was standing at the window of the room, looking out. I saw the reflection in the window, of Elizabeth trying to pick herself up off the floor. She grabbed the chair and lifted with one hand, while still holding the baby with the other. It took me awhile to get around to looking back at my own reflection. As I gazed into the brown eyes staring back at me, I recognized that it was not me. I stood in astonishment for a moment, for the person looking back at me was Luke.

As the images continued a few years later into the future, the mental and physical abuse would eventually take its toll on Elizabeth. And it would ultimately lead her to an early grave. One day, after one of his binge drinking episodes, of things not working out to his satisfaction. Not knowing Elizabeth was carrying the baby, Luke kicked her down a flight of stairs. When Elizabeth woke up in the hospital, she asked for her son. After a few moments of deliberation the doctors finally told her that the child did not survive the altercation. Only a couple of hours after leaving the hospital, Elizabeth grabbed a razor blade from the mirrored cabinet in the bathroom. And with sufficient force, she sliced through the veins in her wrists. In the depths of a great despair and no longer suppressing her own suicidal thoughts, she finished the job that Luke had started many times before, by taking her own life.

"Alright, I've seen enough!" I yelled towards the sky. "Stop the images! I want to go back! I want to go home!" I knew that these visions were not real. I knew that they were of the worst of all possibilities that might happen. Was there a chance that any of this could have happened? Of course, but yet there was also a chance that none of it would ever happen either.

As the dream came to an end, I heard Eddie's voice, yet again. "It is coming William, the time is nearly here. You will have to make your decision and choose your own path now. So be careful and always know I am looking out for you." The words had a lingering echo in my mind as I began contemplating on what to do next. *"I have to somehow find my way out of here."*

"Limbo is no place for you to stay. You must hurry into the light. Go now Will!" I heard Eddie speak for the last time. As another light appeared in from nowhere, I rushed towards and then finally out of the lighted corridor of exaggeration. I was now headed back into the open arms of the substantially insignificant subsist that we all call reality.

Epilogue

"*C*ome on, open your eyes!*" I screamed at myself.

My eye lids were heavy. My body completely weakened from the lifeless out of body experience I had. An immense pressure began in my chest as if I couldn't take in air. My head began to throb as if my brain were about to explode. Tears began to stream down my face as the anxiety began to constrict my throat. I couldn't utter even a single sound as I listened in to the doctor talk to my parents. "We need an answer," she said. "He's doing much better than what Eddie was doing, but the decision is yours. Even if he comes to, at this point we don't know what state of mind he will wake up in."

"I don't know," my mother said in between sobs.

"*No,*" my mind began to scream. "*Don't do this. I just need more time.*"

"We have to," my father chimed in.

"No we don't," my mother continued. "Edward was just wasting away. He progressively got worse with everyday that passed. William, is still fighting in there, I know it."

"Ma'am, with all due respect," the doctor said. "I've seen family's stretch their budgets and time trying to hold on for something that may never happen. First you spend days here at the hospital. Then you start coming to see him every other day, then every week, month, and then you begin a yearly visit. Until you either decide to pull the plug or you move on and forget completely about him."

"See honey," my father said. "We can't just keep extending the unavoidable truth that we will never see him wake up from this. Go ahead Doc, pull the cord."

"Wait," my mother said, "Just one more goodbye." As I felt the warmth of my mother's final embrace, body began to get tense. "William, this is your mother. Life without you and your brother will never be the same for me and your father. Today we made the toughest decisions of our life. Although, it may seem like we are giving up on you. We are not. We are merely giving in to Gods plan. Apparently, you were never meant to live past this point. God must need you and Edward both very much to deprive us of you both. And although you are leaving this Earth prematurely by my own standards; I'm sure God will welcome you with open arms."

"Oh my God," I cried out in my head. *"Hurry up and wake up. So you can slap everyone in the room. Push yourself,"* I continued as my mother and father began to pray for my soul.

"Dear God," my mother prayed. "I know William isn't what you would call a true believer or the meticulousness of a moral boundary like his brother. But he has a strong devotion to what he does believe, and qualities from strength of character that is powerful enough to change the views of the people around him. Find a place for my children in Heaven dear Lord. And grant them and us serenity for our misfortunes. We ask this in Jesus name, Amen."

As she finished I began to breathe more effortlessly. As I stopped for a moment I swallowed and began to speak. "Pull the plug already. If I have to listen to this sappy crap for another minute, I'll kill myself."